'So, do you always go to bed so early?' The moment she had the words out a deep blush bloomed on her cheeks and her lips twisted into a small wince.

Amused at her embarrassment, he couldn't resist saying, 'Only when I have good cause to.'

Her eyes popped open and heat infused her cheeks.

For a moment they just stared at one another, and the atmosphere immediately grew thick with awareness. Two strangers…alone in a house. She was wearing his clothes.

A spark of something happening between them had his pulse firing for the first time in years. And warning bells rang in his ears. She was his neighbour. He was not into relationships. Period. He was no good at them. He had a long day ahead of him. He needed to walk away.

Dear Reader,

I am so thrilled to share *Swept into the Rich Man's World* with you. The inspiration for this story came from a visit to stunning Lough Hyne in West Cork, Ireland.

Lough Hyne is unique, in that it's a seawater lake surrounded by densely wooded hillside. It's ancient and atmospheric, with a hint of magic in the air. Which got me thinking about two people falling in love in such surroundings. Two people who refuse to accept their need for love and friendship.

First I imagined a feisty but wounded woman, determined to get ahead in life on her own terms. What better name to give her than Aideen, a Gaelic word which translates as 'Little Fire'? Then I imagined a resilient, strong man who, buried under the weight of responsibilities, has closed himself off from relationships. And my blue-eyed Irish hero Patrick was born.

As their love story unfolds we move from rural Ireland to Paris, the city of love, where emotions run high and the protective layers they have both built around themselves come undone in the face of love and tenderness.

I have completely fallen in love with Aideen and Patrick, and hope that as you read their journey to love you do too.

Kind regards,

Katrina

SWEPT INTO THE RICH MAN'S WORLD

BY
KATRINA CUDMORE

First published in Great Britain 2016
By Mills & Boon, an imprint of HarperCollins*Publishers*
1 London Bridge Street, London, SE1 9GF

© 2016 Katrina Cudmore

ISBN: 978-0-263-26363-3

Our policy is to use papers that are natural, renewable and recyclable
products and made from wood grown in sustainable forests. The logging
and manufacturing processes conform to the legal environmental
regulations of the country of origin.

Printed and bound in Great Britain
by CPI Antony Rowe, Chippenham, Wiltshire

A city-loving book addict, peony obsessive **Katrina Cudmore** lives in Cork, Ireland, with her husband, four active children and a very daft dog. A psychology graduate, with a MSc in Human Resources, Katrina spent many years working in multinational companies and can't believe she is lucky enough now to have a job that involves daydreaming about love and handsome men!

You can visit Katrina at katrinacudmore.com.

Swept into the Rich Man's World

is Katrina Cudmore's first **Mills & Boon Romance** title.

Visit the Author Profile page at millsandboon.co.uk.

This book is dedicated to my mum.
I miss you with all my heart.

CHAPTER ONE

'HELLO? IS ANYONE HOME?'

Her lungs on fire, Aideen Ryan desperately heaved in some air as she waited for someone to answer her knock and call. She had run in the dark through gale-force winds and rain to get to Ashbrooke House: the only place that could give her shelter from the storm currently pounding the entire Atlantic coastline of Ireland.

Ashbrooke House, stately home of billionaire Patrick Fitzsimon. A man who, given the impenetrable walls that surrounded his vast estate and his über-wealthy lifestyle, was unlikely to welcome her intrusion.

She straightened her rain jacket and ran a hand through her hair. *Oh, for crying out loud.* Her hair was a tangled mess. Soaked to the skull and resembling a frizz bomb... She really hoped it wouldn't be Patrick Fitzsimon who answered the door. Not the suave, gorgeous man she had seen in countless magazines. A man who stared at the camera with such serious intensity and intelligence that she had held her breath in alarm, worried for a few crazy seconds that he could see her spying on him.

The only sightings anyone ever made of him locally was when he was helicoptered in and out of the estate. Intrigued, she had looked him up. But just because she'd been unable to resist checking out her neighbour, one of the world's 'top ten most eligible billionaire bachelors', it didn't alter the fact that she was determined to keep her life a man-free zone.

A nearby tree branch creaked loudly as a ferocious gust of wind and rain swept up from the sea. How was her poor cottage faring in the storm without her? And how on earth was her business going to survive this?

Pushing down her spiralling panic, she took hold of the brass knocker and rapped it against the imposing door again, the metal vibrating against her skin.

'Hello? Please…I need help. Is anyone home?'

Please, please, let one of his staff answer.

But the vast house remained in silence, while beyond the columned entrance porch sheets of rain swept across the often written about formal gardens of Ashbrooke.

And then slow realisation dawned. Although outside lighting had showcased the perfect symmetry and beauty of the Palladian house as she had run up the driveway, not a single interior light had shone through the large sash windows.

In her panic, that simple fact had failed to register with her…until now.

What if nobody was at home?

But that didn't make sense. A house this size had to have an army of staff. The classically inspired villa had a three-storey central block, connected by colonnades to two vast wings. The house was enormous—even bigger than the pictures suggested.

Somebody simply *had* to be home. They probably just couldn't hear her above the storm. She needed to knock louder.

She grabbed hold of the knocker again, but just as

she raised it high to pound it down on the door the door swung open. As she flew forward with it all she could see was a tanned, muscular six-pack vanishing beneath a grey sweatshirt, its owner in the midst of quickly dressing. But not before she headbutted that glorious vision of masculine perfection.

It was like colliding against steel. As she ricocheted backwards she heard a loud grunt. Then hands gripped her upper arms and yanked her back from slamming bottom first on to the ground. The momentum pulled her back towards that hard body, and this time her forehead landed heavily on the person's chest with a thud.

For a moment neither of them moved, and her already spinning head became lost in a giddy sensation of warmth, the safe embrace of another human being, the deep, masculine scent of a man...

She couldn't tell who sprang away first, but as embarrassment barrelled through her, her eyes dropped down to bare feet and dark grey sweatpants before travelling back up over a long, lean, muscular body. Dark stubble lined a sculpted jawline. Taking a deep swallow, she looked up into eyes that were the light blue of an early-morning Irish spring sky. How often had she tried without success to replicate that colour in her designs?

Patrick Fitzsimon.

Those beautiful blue eyes narrowed. 'What the—?'

'I'm sorry I woke you, but my home's been flooded and everything I own is probably floating to America at this stage. I tried to drive into Mooncoyne but the road is flooded. My car got stuck. I was so glad your gates were open...I thought they would be locked, like they usually are. I honestly didn't know what I was going to do if they were locked.'

He held up a hand in the universal *stop* position. 'Okay. Slow down. Let's start again. Explain to me who you are.'

Oh, why did she jabber so much when she was nervous? And, for crying out loud, did she *have* to blush so brightly that she could light up a small house?

Pushing her hand out towards him, she said, 'I'm Aideen Ryan. I'm your neighbour. I live in Fuchsia Cottage…down by the edge of the lough.'

He gave a quick nod of recognition, but then he drew his arms across his impossibly wide chest and his gaze narrowed even more. 'What is it you need, exactly?'

Humiliation burnt in her chest at having to ask for help from a stranger, but she looked into his cool blue eyes and blurted out what had to be said. 'I need a place to stay tonight.'

His mouth twisted unhappily. For a moment she feared he was about to close the door on her.

But instead he took a backward step and said, 'Come inside.'

At best, it was a very reluctant invitation.

The door closed behind them with a solid clunk. Without uttering a word, he left her standing alone in the vast entrance hall. Her body started to shake as her wet clothes clung to her limbs. Her teeth chattered in the vast space and, to her ears, seemed to echo off the dome-shaped ceiling, from which hung the largest crystal chandelier she'd ever seen.

Why couldn't she have a normal neighbour? Why did hers have to be a billionaire who lived in a palace at the end of a mile-long driveway? She hated having to ask for help. From anyone. But having to ask for help from a megarich gorgeous man made her feel as though the universe was having a good laugh at her expense.

When he returned, he passed her a yellow and white striped towel without comment. Accepting it gratefully, she patted her hands and face. For a moment their eyes met.

Her heart stuttered as his gaze assessed her, his generous mouth flattened into a grimace, his long legs planted wide apart, his body rigid. Her breath caught. She felt intimidated by the intensity of his stare, his size, his silent unsmiling presence. She lowered her gaze and concentrated on twisting the towel through her hair, her eyes closing as an unaccountable nervousness overtook her.

'So where's your car?'

'I tried to drive into Mooncoyne but the river had burst its banks at Foley's Bridge. It's the same on your estate—the bridge on your drive is impassable, too.'

He shook his head in confusion. 'So how did you get here?'

'I climbed on to the bridge wall and crawled along it… My car is still on the other side.'

Just great. Not only had he been woken from a jet-lagged sleep, but now he realised he was dealing with a crazy woman. This was all he needed.

'Are you serious? Are you telling me you climbed over a flooded river in gale-force winds? Have you lost your mind?'

For a moment a wounded look flashed in her cocoa-brown eyes, but then she stared defiantly back at him.

'The sea was about to flood my cottage. I called the emergency services but they are swamped with the flooding throughout Mooncoyne. And anyway they can't reach here—Foley's Bridge is impassable even to them. You're my only neighbour. There was no other place I could come to for shelter.' Throwing her head back, she took a deep breath before she continued, a tremor in her voice. 'I did contemplate staying in my car overnight, but frankly I was more concerned about hypothermia than climbing along a bridge wall.'

Okay, so she had a point. But it had still been a crazy risk to take.

He inhaled a deep breath. For the first time ever he wished his staff resided in the house. If she'd been here, his housekeeper, Maureen, would happily have taken this dishevelled woman in hand. And he could have got some much-needed sleep.

He had awoken to her knocking jet-lagged and perplexed as to how anyone had got past his security. All of Ashbrooke's thousand-acre parkland was ring-fenced by a twenty-foot stone wall, built at the same time as the house in the eighteenth century. The impenetrable wall and the electronic front gates kept the outside world away.

Well, they were *supposed* to.

He would be having words with his estate manager in the morning. But right now he had a stranger dripping water down on to his polished limestone floor. He had an urgent teleconference in less than four hours with Hong Kong. To be followed up with a day of endless other teleconferences to wrap up his biggest acquisition ever. The acquisition, however, was still mired in legal and technical difficulties. Difficulties his teams should have sorted out weeks ago. The arrival of his neighbour at this time of night was the last thing he needed.

He glanced at her again. She gave him a brief uncertain smile. And he did a double take. Beneath that mass of wild, out-of-control hair she was beautiful.

Full Cupid's bow lips, clear rosy skin, thick arched

eyebrows and the most expressive eyes he had ever seen, framed by long dark eyelashes. Not the striking, almost hard supermodel beauty of some of his exes. She was... really pretty.

But then with a twinge of guilt he realised that she was shivering, and that she had noticeably paled in the past few minutes.

'You need to get out of those wet clothes and have a shower.'

A glimmer of heat showed on her cheeks and she shuffled uneasily. 'I don't have any spare clothes. I didn't pack any. I only had time to get some office equipment and files out...the things I had to save.'

Oh, great. Well, he didn't have any spare women's clothes hanging around here. He had never brought any of his dates to Ashbrooke. This was his sanctuary. And it had become even more so in the past few years as his ever-growing business demanded his absolute concentration.

Deep down he knew he should say some words of comfort to her. But he was no good in these situations, at saying the right thing. God knew his history with his own sister, Orla, proved that. His skill in life was making money. It clearly wasn't having effective personal relationships.

The thought of how he had failed not only Orla but also his mum and dad left a bitter taste in his mouth as his eyes moved up to meet his neighbour's. Two pools of wary brown met him. He could provide this woman with practical help. But nothing more.

'Pass me your jacket and I'll show you to a guest bedroom. I'll find you some clothes to wear while you shower.'

Her hands trembled as she shrugged off her pink and red floral rain jacket. Beneath it she wore a red and white striped cotton top, a short denim miniskirt, black wool tights and Converse trainers. Not exactly clothing suitable for being outdoors in the midst of an Atlantic storm.

The wet clothes clung to her skin. Despite himself he let his gaze trail down the soft curves of her body, gliding over the gentle slope of her breasts, narrow waist and along the long length of her legs.

When he looked up she gave a shrug. 'I didn't have time to get changed.'

She must have mistaken his stare of appreciation for incredulity. Good. He certainly didn't want her getting any other ideas.

He took her coat and in silence they walked up the stairs.

He glanced briefly at his watch. He would show her to her room and then go and get some sleep. He needed to be at the top of his game tomorrow, to unravel this mess his acquisition teams seemed incapable of sorting out.

She followed him up a cantilevered stone staircase. Despite her longing to get changed out of her rain-soaked clothes—not least her trainers, which squelched with every step—she couldn't help but stop and stare at the opulent rococo plasterwork that curved along the walls of the staircase. Exquisite delicate masks and scallop shells rendered in porcelain-like plaster had her longing to reach out and touch the silent angelic faces, which seemed to follow her steps with knowing smiles.

It was one of the most stunning rooms she had ever seen…if you could call a hallway a room. Good Lord, if the entrance hall was like this what was the rest of the house like? *Talk about making a girl feel inadequate...*

Ahead of her he continued to climb the stairs, his tall, broad frame causing an unwanted flip in her stomach. He was big, dark, and handsome beyond belief. And you didn't need to be Sherlock Holmes to figure out that he wasn't too keen on having her here.

Well, she wasn't too keen on being here herself. She'd much prefer to be at home, snuggled up in her own bed. Having to face the displeasure of a billionaire who, given his monumental success at such a young age, was probably hard-nosed and cold-hearted, was not exactly her idea of a fun night.

Upstairs, he led her down a never-ending corridor in silence. She had an insane urge to talk, to kill the tension that seemed to simmer silently between them.

'Your helicopter often passes over my cottage. Do you travel a lot?'

'When required.'

Okay, so it hadn't been the most interesting or insightful of questions, but he could have given a little more detail in the way of an answer. It wouldn't kill him to make a little small talk with her, would it?

He stopped and opened a door, and signalled for her to enter first. As she passed he studied her with a coolness that gave nothing away. She found herself giving him an involuntary smile. But when his face remained impassive, apart from the slight narrowing of his eyes, she felt rather silly.

His cool attitude pinged in her brain like a wake-up call. She was here out of necessity, not because she wanted to be, and he shouldn't be making her feel so uneasy. She straightened her back with resolve and pride and marched further into the room. First thing tomorrow morning she was out of here.

But she hadn't gone far when her steps faltered. 'Oh, wow, this bedroom is stunning…and it's *huge!* A family of six could easily sleep in that bed.'

An imposing oversized bed sat in the middle of the room, surrounded by sofas and occasional chairs covered in glazed cotton in varying tones of sage-green. An antique desk and a vanity table sat either side of the white marble fireplace.

He didn't acknowledge her words of admiration but instead made for the door. 'I'll go and get you some clothes to change into.'

When he was gone she pulled a face. Did she really have to sound so gushing? Right—from here on in she was playing it cool with Patrick Fitzsimon.

Two doors led to a bathroom and a dressing room. In the bathroom she eyed the shower longingly. She didn't suppose he would be too impressed to return to find her already in the locked bathroom, the shower running, making herself at home…

This was all so horribly awkward. Barging in on a very reluctant neighbour at this time of night…

But then a giggle escaped as she imagined his expression if he returned to a closed bathroom door and, beyond it, the sound of her voice belting out a show tune inside the running shower.

Her laughter died, though, when she walked back out into the bedroom to be confronted with the exact frown she had imagined. As she reddened he threw her a stark look.

'Is something the matter?'

'No…it's just that my wet shoes are making the sound of a sickly duck whenever I walk.'

Oh, for crying out loud. So much for playing it cool. Where had *that* come from?

He looked at her as though he was concerned about her sanity. With a quick shake of his head he placed the bundle in his hands on to one of the fireside chairs. 'Have a shower and get changed. You'll need to wash and dry your clothes for when you leave in the morning. There's a laundry room at the end of this corridor—please use that.'

With that, he turned away. His back was still turned to her when she heard him say goodnight.

'Is it okay if I get myself a drink after I shower?'

He slowed at her question and for a fraction too long he paused, a new tension radiating across his broad shoulders.

When he turned she shrugged and gave an apologetic smile. 'I could really do with something to warm me up. If you tell me how to get to the kitchen, I'll pop down there after.'

Cue a deepening of his grimace. Just for a moment she wondered how gorgeous he must be when he smiled, because he was pretty impressive even when grimacing. *If* he ever smiled, that was.

'Turn left outside the bedroom door and you will find another set of stairs a little further along that will take you down to the west wing. The kitchen is the fifth door on the left.'

He twisted away and was gone before she could voice her thanks.

She exhaled heavily. Was he this abrasive with everyone, or was it her in particular?

God knew she had met plenty of curt people in her

line of business, but there was something about Patrick Fitzsimon that completely threw her. In his company she felt as though an invisible wall separated them. She got on with most people—she was good at putting them at ease. But with him she got the distinct feeling that getting on with people was pretty low on his agenda.

On the bed, she unfurled his bundle: soft grey cotton pyjama bottoms and a pale blue shirt, wrapped around a toothbrush and toothpaste.

Her heart did a funny little shimmy at the thought of wearing his clothes, and before she knew what she was doing she brought them to her nose. Her eyes closed as she inhaled the intoxicating smell of fresh laundry, but there was no hint of the scent she had inhaled earlier when she'd fallen against him. Salt and grass…and a deep, hot, masculine scent that had her swallowing a sigh in remembrance. For a few crazy seconds earlier she had wanted to wrap her arms around his waist. Take shelter against his hardness for ever.

She threw her eyes upwards. What was she doing? The man was as cold as ice.

Anyway, it didn't matter. After tomorrow she would probably never see him again. And she was not interested in men right now anyway. Her hard-won independence was too precious. From here on in she wanted to live a life in which she was in charge of her own destiny. Where *she* called the shots.

One night and she was out of here. Back to her work and back to nights in, eating pizza and watching box sets on her own. Which she was perfectly happy with, thank you very much.

CHAPTER TWO

SIXTEEN BEDROOMS, EIGHT reception rooms. A ballroom that could cater to over three hundred guests. Two libraries and countless other rooms he rarely visited. And yet he resented the idea of having to share this vast house with someone. He knew it made no sense. It was almost midnight. She would be gone within hours. But, after spending the past few years immersed in the solitude of his work, having to share his home even for one night was an alien and uncomfortable prospect.

Two years ago, after yet another bewildering argument with his sister, he had come to the realisation that he should focus on what he was good at, what he could control: his work. He had been exhausted and frustrated by Orla's constant battle of wills with him, and it had been almost a relief to turn away from the fraught world of relationships to the uncomplicated black and white world of work.

He hadn't needed Orla to tell him he was inept at handling relationships, though she happily did so on a regular basis, because he'd seen it in the pain etched on her face when she didn't realise he was watching her.

He still didn't know what had gone wrong. Where *he* had gone wrong. They had once been so close. After his mum had died he had been so scared and lonely he had thought his heart would break. But the smiling, gurgling Orla had saved him.

And then his father had died when Orla was sixteen, and almost overnight she had changed. She had gone from being happy-go-lucky to sullen and non-communicative, and their once unbreakable bond had been broken.

The scrape of a tree branch against the kitchen window pane brought him back to the present with a jolt.

He put the tea canister next to the already boiled kettle. Then he wrote his house guest a quick note, telling her to help herself to anything she needed. All the while he was hearing his father's incredulous voice in his head, scolding him for his inhospitality. And once again he was reminded of how different he was from his father.

Note finished, he knew he should walk away before she came down. But the image of her standing in his entrance hall, a raindrop running down over the deep crevice of her full lips, held him. Lips he had had an insane urge to taste…

His instant attraction to her had to be down to the fact that he had been without a steady bedmate for quite some time. A lifetime for a guy who had once never been able to resist the lure of a beautiful woman. But two years ago his appetite for his usual short, frivolous affairs had disappeared. And a serious relationship was off the cards. Permanently.

And, anyway, she was his neighbour. If—and it was a big *if*—he ever was to start casually dating again, it certainly wouldn't be on his own doorstep.

He turned at a soft knock on the door.

Standing at the entrance to the vast kitchen, she gave him a wary smile.

He should have gone when he could. Now he would be forced to make small talk.

She had rolled up the cuffs of his pyjama bottoms and shirt and her feet were bare. He got the briefest glimpse of a delicate shin bone, which caused a tightening in his belly in a way it never should. Her hair, though still wet, was now tamed and fell like a heavy dark curtain down her back. For a moment his eyes caught on how she had left the top two buttons of the shirt undone, and although he could only see a small triangle of flesh his pulse quickened.

He didn't want to be feeling any of this. He crumpled the note he had left her into the palm of his hand. 'The kettle is boiled. Please help yourself to anything you need.'

'Thank you.' As he went to walk to the door she added, 'I didn't say it earlier, but thank you for giving me shelter for the night—and I'm sorry if I woke you up.'

She blushed when she'd finished, and wound her arms about her waist, eyeing him cautiously. There was something about her standing there in his clothes, waiting for his response, that got to him.

He felt compelled to hold out an olive branch. 'In the morning I will arrange for my estate manager to drive you home.'

She shook her head firmly. 'I'll walk. It's not far to the bridge.'

'Fine.'

It was time for him to go and get some sleep. But something was holding him back. Perhaps it was his thoughts of Orla, and how he would like someone to treat *her* if she was in a similar predicament.

With a heavy sigh he said, 'How about we start again?'

Her head tilted to the side and she bit her lip, unsure.

He walked over to her and held out his hand and said words that, in truth, he didn't entirely mean. 'Welcome to Ashbrooke.'

Her hand was ice-cold. Instinctively he coiled his own around the soft, delicate skin as gently as he could.

'You're cold.'

Her head popped up from where she had been staring at their enclosed hands and when she spoke there was a tremble in her voice that matched the one in her hand. 'I know. The shower helped a little, but I was wet to the bone. I've never seen a storm like it before.'

He crossed over to the cloakroom, situated just off the kitchen, and grabbed one of the heavy fleeces he used for horse riding.

Back in the kitchen, he handed her the fleece.

'Thank you. I…' Her voice trailed off and her gaze wandered behind him before her mouth broke into a wide glorious smile. 'Oh—hello, you two.'

He twisted around to find the source of her affection. His two golden Labs had left their beds in the cloakroom and now ambled towards her, tails wagging at the prospect of having someone else to love them.

Both immediately went to her and bumped their heads against her leg. She leant over and rubbed them vigorously. In the process of her doing so her shirt fell forward and he got a brief glimpse of the smooth swell of her breasts. She was not wearing a bra.

Blood pounded in his ears. It was definitely time for bed.

'They're gorgeous. What are their names?'

'Mustard and Mayo.'

Raising an eyebrow, she gave him a quick grin. 'Interesting choice of names.'

A sputter of pleasure fired through him at the teasing in her voice. And he experienced a crazy urge to keep this brief moment of ease between them going. But that didn't make sense, so instead he said curtly, 'Remind me of your name again?'

Her eyes grew wide and her cheeks reddened. With a low groan she threw her hands up in the air. 'I *knew* it. I woke you up, didn't I?'

He folded his arms. 'Maybe I'm just terrible at remembering people's names?'

Her eyes narrowed shrewdly. 'I doubt that very much.' And then she added, 'So, do you always go to bed so early?'

The moment she had the words out an even deeper blush bloomed on her cheeks and her lips twisted into a small wince.

Something fired in his blood. 'Only when I have good cause to.'

Her mouth fell open.

For a moment they just stared at one another, and the atmosphere immediately grew thick with awareness. Two strangers, alone in a house. She was wearing his clothes. The spark of something happening between them had his pulse firing for the first time in years. And warning bells rang in his ears. She was his neighbour. He was not into relationships. Period. He was no good at them. He had a long day ahead of him. He needed to walk away.

A coil of heat grew in Aideen's belly.

Propped against an antique wing-backed chair, in the low light of the kitchen, Patrick looked at her with an edgy darkness. She stood close by, her back to the island unit. She dropped her gaze to the small sprigs of flowers on the material covering the chair, instantly recognising the signature motif of a luxurious French textile manufacturer. Everything in this house was expensive, out of her league. Including its owner.

She should talk, but her pulse was beating way too quickly for her to formulate a sensible sentence. He went to stand up, and his movement prompted her to blurt out, 'Aideen Ryan… My name is Aideen Ryan.'

Rather reluctantly he held out his hand. 'And I'm Patrick Fitzsimon.'

Thrown by the way her heart fluttered once again at the touch of his hand, she said without thinking, 'Oh, I know that.'

'Really?'

For a moment she debated whether she could bluster her way out of the situation, but one look into his razor-sharp eyes told her she would be wasting her time. 'Every time I drove by I was intrigued as to who lived here, so I looked you up one day.'

His expression tightened.

She realised she must sound like some billionaire groupie or, worse, a gold digger, and blurted out, 'We *are* the only houses out here on the headland. I wanted to know who my only neighbour was. There was nothing else to it.'

After a torturous few seconds during which he considered her answer, he said, 'I'll ask my estate manager to drop down to you tomorrow. He can give you his contact details. That way if you ever need any help you can contact him directly.'

For a few seconds she smiled at him gratefully, but

then humiliation licked at her bones. He was putting a filter between them. But then what did she expect? Patrick Fitzsimon lived in the moneyed world of the super-rich. He wasn't interested in his neighbours.

'Thanks, but I'm able to cope on my own.'

He stood up straight and scowled at her. 'I didn't say you weren't.'

She gave a tight laugh, memories of her ex taunting her. 'Well, you're not like a lot of men, then...'

The scowl darkened even more. 'That's a bit of a sweeping statement, isn't it? I was only trying to be helpful.'

The last sentence had been practically growled. He looked really angry with her, and she couldn't help but think she had hit a raw nerve.

She inhaled a deep breath and said, 'I'm sorry...I'm a bit battle-scarred at the moment.'

He stared at her in surprise and, praying he wouldn't ask her what she meant, she said quickly, 'I don't know about you, but I could do with a cup of tea. Will you join me?'

He looked as taken aback by her invitation as she was. Did she *really* want to spend more time with this taciturn man? But after the night she'd had, and three months of living alone, the truth was she was starved for company.

He looked down at his watch and when he looked up again frowned at her in thought. 'I'll stay five minutes.'

Could he have said it with any *less* enthusiasm? He looked edgy. As though he wanted to escape.

He walked towards the countertop where the kettle stood. 'Take a seat at the table. If you prefer, I also have hot chocolate or brandy.'

'Thanks, but I'd love tea.'

Instead of going to the table she walked to the picture window in the glass extension at the side of the kitchen. The faint flashing light from the lighthouse out on the end of the headland was the only sight in the darkness of the stormy night.

'Do you think my cottage will be okay?'

He didn't answer immediately. Instead he walked over to her side and he, too, looked out of the window towards the lighthouse. In the reflection of the window she could see that he stood four, maybe five inches taller than her, his huge frame dwarfing hers.

'I called the emergency services when you were in the shower. I really don't know what will happen to your cottage. The timing of the storm surge was terrible—right at the same time as high tide. I thought the worst of the storms was over, but April can be an unpredictable month.' He turned slightly towards her. 'I know you must be worried—it's your home—but you're safe. That's all that matters.'

His words surprised her, and she had to swallow against the lump of emotion that formed in her throat. He didn't try to pretend everything would be okay, didn't lie to her, but he didn't dismiss how she was feeling either.

She gave him a grateful smile, but he looked away from her with a frown.

He moved away from the window, back towards the table, and said in a now tight voice, 'Your tea is ready.'

For a while she looked down at the mug tentatively, two forces battling within her. The need to be self-reliant was vying with her need to talk to someone—even someone as closed-off as Patrick Fitzsimon. To hear a little reassurance that things would be okay. And then she just blurted it out, the tension in her body easing fractionally as the words tumbled out.

'It's not just my cottage, though. My studio is there. I have some urgent work I have to complete. I missed a deadline today and I have another commissioned piece I need to deliver next week.'

His silence and his frown told her she had said too much, and her insides curled with embarrassment. The man was a billionaire. Her problems must seem trivial to him.

She twisted her mug on the table, knowing he was studying her but unable to meet his gaze.

'I'm sorry to hear that. I didn't realise. What is it that you do?'

'I'm a textile designer.'

He nodded, and his eyes held hers briefly before he looked away. 'Try not to think about work until tomorrow. You might be worrying for no reason... And even in the worst of situations there's always a solution.'

'Hopefully you're right.'

'Do you have anyone who can help you tomorrow?'

She shook her head. 'I haven't got to know people locally yet, and my family live in Dublin. Most of my friends are either there or in London.'

Realising she still hadn't touched her tea, she sipped it. In her nervousness she pulled the mug away too quickly and had to lick a falling drip of tea from her bottom lip.

Her heart somersaulted as she saw his eyes were trained on her mouth, something darkening in their intensity. Then very slowly his gaze moved up to capture hers. Awareness fluttered through her.

'I heard someone had bought Fuchsia Cottage late last year—why did you move here to Mooncoyne?'

He asked the question in an almost accusatory tone, as though he almost wished she hadn't.

'I saw the cottage and the studio online and I fell in love with them straight away. The cottage is adorable, and the studio space is incredible. It's perfect for my work.' Forcing herself to smile, she said, 'Unfortunately I hadn't bargained on the cottage and studio flooding. The auctioneer assured me it wouldn't.'

He gave a brief shrug of understanding. 'You weren't tempted to go back to your family in Dublin?'

'Have you seen the price of property in Dublin? I know it's not as bad as London, but it's still crazy.' Then, remembering who she was talking to, she felt her insides twist and a feeling of foolishness grip her. Clearing her throat, she asked, 'Has Ashbrooke always been in your family?'

He looked at her incredulously, as though her question was ridiculous. 'No...absolutely not. I grew up in a modest house. My family weren't wealthy.'

Taken aback by the defensive tone of his voice, she blurted out exactly what was on her mind. 'So how did all of this happen?'

He studied her with a blistering glance, his mouth a thin line of unhappiness. In the end he said curtly, 'I was lucky. I saw the opportunities available in mobile applications ahead of the curve. I developed some music streaming apps that were bought by some of the big internet providers. Afterwards I had the capital to invest in other applications and software start-ups.'

She couldn't help but shake her head and give him a mock sceptical look. 'Oh, come on—that wasn't luck.'

'Meaning...?'

'Look, I ran my own business for five years. I know

success is down to hard work, taking risks, and being constantly on the ball. Making smart business decisions…I reckon luck has very little to do with it.'

'All true. But sometimes you get a good roll of the dice—sometimes you don't. It's about getting back up when things go wrong, knowing there's always a solution to a problem.'

His words were said with such certainty they unlocked something inside her.

For a good few minutes she toyed with her mug. The need to speak, to *tell* him, was building up in her like a pressure cooker. Part of her felt ridiculous, thinking of telling a billionaire of her failings, but another part wanted to. Why, she wasn't sure. Maybe it was the freedom of confessing to a stranger? To a person she wouldn't see after tomorrow? Perhaps it was not being able to talk to her family and friends about it because she had got it all so wrong.

'I lost my business last year,' she said in a rush.

Non-judgemental eyes met hers, and he said in a tone she hadn't heard from him before, 'What happened?'

Taken aback by the softening in him, she hesitated. Her pulse began to pound. Suddenly her throat felt bone-dry. 'Oh, it's a long story, but I made some very poor business decisions.'

'But you're back? Trying again.'

He said it with such certainty, as though that was all that mattered, and she couldn't help but smile. Something lifted inside her at the knowledge he was right. Yes, she was trying again—trying hard. Just hearing him say it made her realise how true it was.

'Yes, I am.'

His serious, intelligent gaze remained locked on hers. 'What are your plans for the future?'

His question caused a flutter of anxiety and her hands clenched on the mug. She shuffled in her seat. For some reason she wanted to get this right. She wanted his approval.

She inhaled a deep breath and said, 'To build a new label, re-establish my reputation.' She cringed at the wobble in her voice; it was just that she was so desperate to rebuild the career she loved so much.

He leant across the table and fixed his gaze on her. It was unnerving to be captivated by those blue eyes. By the sheer size and strength of him as his arms rested on the table, his broad shoulders angled towards her.

'There's no shame in failing, Aideen.'

Heat barrelled through her and she leant back in her chair, away from him. 'Really?' She pushed her mug to the side. 'What would *you* know about failing?'

His jaw hardened, and when he spoke his low voice was harsh with something she couldn't identify.

'Trust me—I have failed many times in my life. I'm far from perfect.'

She looked at him sceptically. He looked pretty perfect to her. From his financial stability and security and his film-star looks to this beautiful house, everything *was* perfect...even his spotless kitchen.

He stood and grabbed both mugs. With his back to her he said, 'I think it's time we went to bed.'

Once again he was annoyed with her. She should leave it. Go to bed, as he had suggested. But curiosity got the better of her. 'Why are you here in Mooncoyne? Why not somewhere like New York or London?'

He turned and folded his arms, leant against the counter. 'I met the previous owner of Ashbrooke, Lord Balfe, at a dinner party in London and we became good friends. He invited me to stay here and I fell in love with the house and the estate. Lord Balfe couldn't afford the upkeep any longer, and he was looking to sell the estate to someone who felt as passionate as he did about conserving it. So I agreed to buy it.' His unwavering eyes held hers and he said matter-of-factly, 'My business was growing ever more demanding. I knew I needed to live somewhere quiet in order to focus on it. This estate seemed the perfect place. And also Mooncoyne reminded me of the small fishing village where I grew up in County Antrim.'

So *that* was why he had traces of a soft, melodic Northern Irish brogue. 'Do your family still live there?'

Another quick look at his watch. He flicked his gaze back up to her. He looked as though he wasn't going to answer, but then he took her by surprise and said, 'No, my mum died when I was a boy and my dad passed away a number of years ago.'

For a moment their eyes locked and incomprehensively she felt tears form at the back of hers. 'I'm sorry.'

Blue eyes held hers and her pulse quickened at the intimacy of looking into a stranger's eyes for more than a polite second or two. Not being able to look away...not wanting to look away.

Then his hands gripped the countertop and he dipped his head for a moment before he looked back up and spoke. 'It happens. I have a younger sister, Orla, who lives in Madrid.'

'Do you see her often?'

His mouth twisted unhappily. 'Occasionally.'

His tone told her to back off. Tension filled the room.

She hated an unhappy atmosphere. And she didn't want to cause him any offence.

So, in a bid to make amends and lighten the tension, she said what she had been thinking all night. 'You've a spectacularly beautiful home.'

He gave a brief nod of acknowledgement. 'Thank you. I'm very proud of the work we've done here over the past few years.'

'How many staff do you employ?'

'I've cleaning and housekeeping staff who come in every day. Out on the estate my estate manager, William, employs twenty-two staff between the stables and the farm.'

'No housekeeper...even a butler?'

His mouth lifted ever so slightly. If she had blinked she would have missed it.

'Sorry to disappoint you but I like my privacy. And I can cook for myself, do up my own buttons, tie my own shoelaces...'

She knew she was pushing it, but decided to push her luck as curiosity got the better of her. 'A girlfriend?' She tried to ignore the unexpected stab of jealousy that came with the thought that there might be a special woman in his life.

Something dark flashed in his eyes and he quietly answered. 'No—no girlfriend.'

She tried to fill the silence that followed. 'So nobody but you lives in the house?'

'No. Now, I think it's time for bed.'

So they were all alone tonight. It shouldn't matter, but for some reason heat grew in her belly at that thought. This was a huge place for one man to live in alone.

Though she stood in preparation for leaving the

kitchen she didn't move away from the table. Instead she said, 'Wow. Don't you get lonely?'

'I prefer to live on my own. I don't have time for re-lationships.' He studied her sombrely. 'Why? Do *you* get lonely?'

Taken aback, she answered, 'I'm too busy. I can—'

A tightness in her chest stopped her mid-sentence. Maybe she *had* been lonely these past few months, and had been denying it all along in her determination to get her business back up and running again.

She shrugged and looked at him with a half smile. 'I must admit it's nice to talk to someone face to face for a change, rather than on the phone or over the internet. I seem to spend all my days on the phone at the moment, calling prospective clients.' With a sigh of exasperation she added, 'I really should go and visit them. It would save me a lot of time being put on hold.'

'Why don't you?'

She felt herself blush. 'Most of my clients are based in Paris, and it's on my list of priorities to visit them.' She couldn't admit that financially she wasn't in a position to travel there, so instead she said, 'But, to be honest, part of me is embarrassed. I haven't seen any of them since I lost my business. I suppose my pride has taken a dent.'

'Go back out there and be proud that you're back and fighting. *I'm* going to Paris next week...' He didn't finish the sentence and a look of annoyance flashed across his face. His tone now cooler, he said, 'You have a long day ahead of you tomorrow. I'll walk you back to your room.'

He called to the dogs and led them back to their beds in the cloakroom.

As they approached the bottom of the stairs she gave him a smile and offered him her hand. 'Thank you for tonight.' A surprising lump of something had formed in her throat, and her voice was croaky when she finally managed to continue to speak. 'Thank you for taking me in. I plan on leaving early tomorrow, so in case I don't see you then, it was nice to meet you.'

Tension seemed to bounce off the surrounding walls and she felt dizzy when his hand took hers. 'I wake before dawn, so the security alarm will be disabled after that.' With a quick nod he added, 'Take care of yourself.'

He walked away, back towards the main entrance hall.

She walked up the stairs slowly, her head spinning. What on earth had possessed her to tell him so much? And why on earth did the thought that she might never see him again make her feel sad? The man obviously didn't want her in his house.

As she lay in bed the memory of his incredible blue eyes and quiet but assured presence left her twisting and tumbling and wishing the hours away so she could leave for home. Where she could lose herself in her work again.

And when sleep finally started to pull her into oblivion her tired mind replayed on a loop his deep voice saying, 'You're safe. That's all that matters.' Words he would probably say to anyone. But when he had said them to her, he had looked at her with such intensity it had felt as though he was tattooing them on her heart.

CHAPTER THREE

PATRICK TORE ALONG the bridle path that cut through the woods, pushing his horse harder and harder. Soft ground underfoot, branches whizzing by, the flash of vivid, almost purple patches of bluebells, calm cool air beating against his skin…

When they reached the edge of the woods they raced through the parkland's glistening green grass. They leapt time and time again over the ditches separating the fields. Adrenaline pumped in both man and mare.

They followed the ancient pathway that hugged the coast and galloped in the steps of the medieval pilgrims who had come to Mooncoyne abbey.

The rising sun slatted its thick rays of sunlight through the window openings and he pulled the horse to a halt by the entrance. He dismounted and walked into the nave.

He hadn't managed to get back to sleep again last night. Instead he had lain awake, wondering how his conversation with Aideen Ryan had become so personal so quickly. It had unsettled him. That wasn't how he operated. He didn't open up to anyone.

For crying out loud, he had almost suggested to her that she travel with him to Paris. His guess was that it wasn't just pride standing in her way of going, but also financial difficulties. In the end he had ended the conversation, been glad when she'd made her own way to bed, because he hadn't been able to handle how good it was to talk to someone else, to actually *connect* with them.

And, despite himself, he was deeply attracted to her.

All of which was dangerous.

He threw his head back and stared up into the endless depths of the blue sky.

Hadn't he already proved he wasn't capable of having effective relationships? He had a string of exes who had been beautiful but superficial. A sister who wouldn't talk to him. And a nephew or niece he would never get to know.

The baby would be born in the next month. He should be there. Supporting Orla. At least she was willing to accept his financial support. If she had refused to do so then he really would have been out of his mind, worrying about how she was going to cope.

His call to Hong Kong earlier had gone well. If he kept up the pressure for the remainder of the day, with the rest of his acquisition teams, then the deal would go through later tonight. It would be strange for it all to be over. For months he had worked day and night to see it happen.

A strange emptiness sat in his chest. What would he do once the project was over?

The slow tendrils of an idea had formed in his mind but he kept pushing them away. But as he walked through the ruins of the abbey the idea came back, stronger and more insistent this time.

He should help Aideen. It was what any good neighbour would do. It was what his father would have done.

But would he be crazy to do it? Last night he had lowered his guard around her. He couldn't allow that again. If he was to help then it would have to be done on a strictly business basis. He could help her re-establish her business, mentor her if required. He knew what it was like to throw your heart and soul into a business. And he knew only too well the pain of failure.

He would help her. And it would all be professional and uncomplicated.

The memory of a deep voice snaked through Aideen's brain. She gave a small sigh, smiled to herself, and stretched out on the bed.

But then her eyes popped open and she looked around, disorientated. Small shafts of daylight sneaked under drawn curtains.

Slowly she remembered where she was. And what she had to face today.

Dreaming about Patrick Fitzsimon was the last thing she should be doing.

The cottage. Deadlines.

For a few seconds she pulled the duvet up over her head. Maybe she could just stay here in this warm and dark cocoon for a few days.

With a groan she pushed back the cover. Time to rise and shine. And face what the day had to bring.

Anyway, it couldn't be any worse than being forced out of the business she'd once created. She had survived the past year, so she would survive this.

She pulled the curtains apart and winced as daylight flooded the room.

The view out of her window was breathtaking. Below her, formal box gardens led down to a gigantic fountain that sprayed a sprout of water so vigorously upwards it was as though it was trying to defy gravity. Rose gardens lay beyond the fountain, and then a long rolling meadow, rich in rain-drenched emerald green grass, ran all the way down to the faraway sea.

Though the sun was still low in the sky the light was dazzling, thanks to a startlingly clear blue sky.

Had last night's storm been in her imagination? How could such furious weather be followed by such a beautiful day?

She could almost convince herself maybe her cottage hadn't flooded. That the weather was a good omen. But she had seen the ferocity of the sea. There was no way her cottage had got away with avoiding that angry swell.

When she had come to view the property she had fallen in love with the old cottage and its outbuildings, arranged around a courtyard garden. Fuchsia had dangled from the hedgerows and fading old roses had tumbled from its walls. It had seemed the perfect solution then.

But now her income was sparser and more sporadic than she had projected, and sometimes she wondered whether she could make this work. That was one of the worst consequences of losing her business: the vulnerability and constant questioning of whether she was doing the right thing, making the right decisions.

But a burning passion for her work along with a heavy dose of pride got her through most days. She would sacrifice everything to make this business a success.

Her heart was a different matter, though. It felt bruised. To think that once upon a time she had thought her ex had loved her...

Pressing the edges of her palms against her eyes, she drew in a deep breath.

A quick shower, an even quicker coffee, and she would

head home to start sorting out whatever was waiting for her.

She mightn't even see Patrick. Which would be a *good* thing, right?

Heading to the bathroom, she sighed. Just who was she trying to kid?

The truth was giddiness was fizzing through her veins at the prospect of seeing his tall, muscular body, the darkness of his hair, and his lightly tanned skin which emphasised the celestial blue of his eyes.

Showered and dressed, she was about to open the bedroom door when she spotted a note pushed under it. Picking it up, she read the brief words.

Aideen,
I will drive you back to your cottage. Help yourself to breakfast in the kitchen. I will meet you in the main entrance hall at nine.
Patrick

It was a generous offer, but she needed to face the cottage on her own. It was her responsibility. She had taken up enough of his time as it was.

And then she studied the note again as an uncomfortable truth dawned on her. Was he offering to take her as a way of ensuring that she left? Humiliation burnt on her cheeks.

She checked the time on her phone. It was not yet eight o'clock. She would get changed and then go reassure him that she was leaving and was perfectly capable of making her own way home.

Thirty minutes later she had searched for him throughout the house but there was no sign of him. Her search in this exquisite house, as she'd gasped at the beauty of the baroque ballroom, with its frescoed ceiling, mirrored walls, and golden chandeliers, had brought home how different their lives were.

She was writing a note for him in the kitchen when the cloakroom door swung open.

Over off-white jodhpurs and black riding boots he was wearing a loose pale green shirt, the top three buttons open to reveal a masculine smattering of dark hair. His skin glistened with a sheen of perspiration.

He came to a stop when he spotted her at the table.

'Good morning.' He moved across the kitchen in long strides while adding, 'Help yourself to breakfast. I'll have a quick shower and be ready by nine.'

His manner was brusque, and she was left with no doubt that he just wanted to get the business of taking her home over and done with. Embarrassment coiled its way around her insides and she wanted to curl up into a protective ball against his rejection.

But instead she gave him a sunny smile. 'Thank you for the offer, but there's really no need for you to drive me. I've taken up enough of your time.' He turned to her with a frown and she added, as way of explanation, 'I'll collect my car down by the bridge. I could do with a walk anyway.'

'I'm coming.'

Didn't he trust her? Was he always this insistent?

'No, honestly—you've done enough.'

He leant against the island unit at the centre of the kitchen. 'Aideen, there's no point in arguing. I've made up my mind.'

His cool composure set her teeth on edge. 'I want to go to the cottage by myself.'

'Why?'

Oh, for crying out loud. 'Because I can manage. The cottage is my responsibility. And I have no doubt that you are an extremely busy man. I can't take up any more of your time.'

'I'm taking you. End of story.'

She was leaving. Why wasn't that enough for him? She gave a small laugh and said jokingly, 'You don't have to personally escort me off the estate, you know.'

He obviously didn't enjoy her joke as annoyance flared on his face. 'Do you really think that is why I want to drive you to the cottage? That I want to make sure you leave?'

Thrown by his anger, she challenged him back. 'What other reason could you possibly have?'

His blue gaze held hers for a long time, and then, with a deep inhalation, he said in a quiet voice, 'Why can't you just accept that I want to help you?'

He moved beside the table and hunkered down beside her. Heat coursed through her veins at having his powerful body so close by, at seeing the movement of the hard muscles of his thighs beneath the thin fabric of the jodhpurs, the beauty of his lightly tanned hand and forearm which rested on the table beside her.

He didn't speak again until she met his determined gaze. 'Let me help you.'

Why wasn't he listening to her? She was able to look after herself—she didn't need any help.

'I appreciate the offer, but I can manage by myself.'

He stood, his jaw working, and eyed her unhappily. 'As you wish.'

With that, he strode out of the kitchen without a backward glance.

* * *

For the second time in less than twelve hours Aideen knocked at Patrick's front door. If she'd hated to ask for help the first time around then it was ten times worse now. Talk about having to eat humble pie…

As she waited for her knock to be answered she looked back towards her car. Thankfully it had started immediately, and although the floor was a little damp, the files and office equipment piled on to the back seat and in the boot had escaped the storm and flood waters.

Unlike her cottage.

She needed to think straight, but her mind was pingponging all over the place. Work. Deadlines. Insurance claims. Where would she even start in finding a reputable builder to carry out the necessary repairs?

She turned to the sound of the door opening.

A middle-aged woman stood there, a puzzled look on her face. As though she was surprised to find someone standing at the door. 'Can I help you?'

'Can I speak to Patrick, please?'

The woman looked totally taken aback. To assure her that she wasn't some random stranger, Aideen quickly added, 'I'm Aideen Ryan. I live in Fuchsia Cottage, down by the lough. Your estate manager was at the front gates, repairing them after last night's storm. Patrick had told him how my cottage flooded last night and he let me in when I said I needed to talk to Patrick again.'

'Oh, you poor thing. Of course—come in. Sure, half the village is flooded. I never saw anything like it in my life.'

The woman led her to a large reception room off the entrance hall, chatting all the way.

'You took me by surprise. We don't tend to get many

visitors. Make yourself comfortable and I'll let Patrick know you're here.'

It took Patrick so long to arrive that for a while she worried that he was refusing to see her. He marched into the room, his brow furrowed. He was wearing a light blue formal shirt, open at the neck, fine navy wool trousers and expensive tan-coloured shoes. It all screamed expensive Italian designer and he looked every inch the successful billionaire that he was.

She gave him a crooked smile. 'I'm back.'

His frown didn't budge an inch. 'So I see.'

She took a deep breath. She had to focus on work. A little bit of humility had never killed anyone. 'My cottage is uninhabitable. The insurance company is sending out an assessor tomorrow. I tried to go to Mooncoyne, but Foley's Bridge is still impassable.' Trying not to wince at his deepening frown, she said in a rush, 'I was wondering if it would be possible for me to work from here... until the flooding subsides.'

His head tilted forward and he pinned her with a look.

'It's just that I have a commission I need to complete by the end of today and I need access to the internet.'

'What condition is the cottage in?'

Her stomach lurched, but she clenched her fists and forced herself to speak. 'There's still floodwater in both the cottage and the studio. Most of my furniture and all the fitted furniture will probably need to be replaced. At a guess, and after speaking to the insurance company, I'll be out of the cottage for at least a month.'

She was feigning calmness about the whole situation but she wasn't fooling him. The storm damage was exactly as he had anticipated. He clenched his teeth in frustration.

Why had she been so stubborn in refusing his offer to go with her? He'd had some spare time then. Now he had back-to-back meetings scheduled for the rest of the day.

He would give her fifteen minutes. Get her to see the sense of his plan. And then he would get back to wrapping up this acquisition.

'How about all your personal belongings? Are they okay?'

'All of my clothes survived, but not my shoes—unfortunately.' A sad, crooked smile broke on her mouth before she added in bewilderment, with a catch in her voice, 'I mean, *shoes*! They are the least of my worries... but I loved them so much.'

'Where are you going to live?'

'I'm not sure... I called the Harbour View Hotel but they're completely booked out tonight, and apparently all the bed and breakfasts in a ten-mile radius are the same because of people having to evacuate. I'll probably have to stay in one of the hotels in Ballymore.'

There was no way she was going to manage the renovations from twenty miles away and work on her commissions at the same time.

'It's going to be difficult for you to manage the repairs from Ballymore. I'll get William, my estate manager, to project-manage the renovations for you.'

She stared at him in disbelief. 'Why on earth would you do that?'

'Because you need to concentrate on your business—not spend your days driving all over the countryside and chasing builders.'

'I appreciate the offer, but I need to manage the renovations by myself.'

'Why?'

Tiredly, she rubbed her palms over her face and looked at him imploringly. 'Let me ask you the same question. Why? Why are you doing this?'

Taking a step closer, he stared down at her. Boy, was she obstinate. 'Maybe I just want to help you. Nothing more.'

'I can't accept your help.'

'Why not?'

'Because...'

This woman was impossible. *Why* wouldn't she accept his help? She was as bad as Orla.

He gave an exasperated sigh. 'Aideen, will you stop being a pain and just agree to letting William sort out the renovations...? It's not a big deal. And I don't know about you, but I have better things to be doing than standing here arguing about my motives.'

Not a big deal to him, perhaps, but it was to her. She needed to rebuild her life by herself, on her own terms.

Bewildered, she said, 'You don't even know me.'

'So? You're my neighbour. That's a good enough reason for me to want to help.'

He made it all sound so simple. And for a moment she wanted to believe him. But then a siren of warning sounded in her brain. She needed to be in control of her own life. 'I don't want to sound ungrateful, and I do appreciate your offer, but I have to manage the renovations by myself.'

'And what if your business suffers as a result?'

She flinched at the truth of his words. Ballymore was twenty miles away, on twisting roads. Trying to manage the renovations and run her business from a hotel room was going to be a nightmare.

Frustration at the whole situation had her arguing back. 'I'll manage.'

His mouth tensed at the anger in her voice and he considered her through narrowed eyes. 'You *are* stubborn, aren't you?'

'So it has been said in the past,' she muttered.

On an exasperated exhalation he folded his arms. 'Your business has to be your number one priority. William will sort out the renovations. You will move in here until the cottage is ready, and on Sunday you will come to Paris with me.'

A bolt of pain radiated through his jawline as he clamped his teeth together. Hard. For a few seconds he wondered at the words he had so casually tossed out. Disquiet rumbled in his stomach. Was he about to walk into a minefield of complications by inviting this woman into his life? But in an instant he killed that doubt. This was the right thing to do. She needed his help. Even if the horror in her eyes told him that she wasn't ready to accept it yet.

Stupefied, Aideen stared at him for the longest while, waiting for him to give the tiniest indication that he was joking. But his mouth didn't twitch…his eyes didn't soften.

She gave a laugh of disbelief. 'Are you being serious?'

'Yes. I have meetings in Paris all of next week. You said yourself that you should be out meeting clients. Well, now is your opportunity. I have a chateau close to Paris we can use.'

'But I would be intruding.'

'Look, you've seen the size of Ashbrooke. My chateau outside Paris is large, too. You can set up a temporary studio there for the week. We can keep out of each other's way.'

Shaking her head, she folded her arms across her chest. 'You said last night you like living on your own… and so do I. It won't work.'

'We'll lead our own lives. I'm simply offering you a bed and a place to work—both here and in Paris. You come and go as you please. My chauffeur will be available to you whenever you need him. It doesn't have to be more complicated than that.'

'But *why*?'

'What is it with you and your questions? Why don't you believe that I'm just trying to be a good neighbour? That it's the right thing to do? I admire your tenacity and I want to support you in rebuilding your business. I think you need help even if you are too stubborn to admit it yourself.'

Taken aback by the powerful intensity of his words, she wavered a little. 'I'd pay you back.'

Taking a deep breath, he said with exasperation, 'I don't want your money. Can't you just accept it as a neighbourly gesture?'

'I'll be paying rent.'

He held up his hands. 'Fine. You can pay me once your insurance money comes through. Now I need to get back to work. I'll show you to the library, where you can work today. Use the same bedroom as last night to sleep in.' Out in the corridor, he added, 'You met my housekeeper, Maureen, earlier. Speak to her if you need anything. I'll get William to call in to see you and together you can discuss the renovation plans.'

She followed him to the library. Was she crazy to agree to this? But it was the only sensible option open to her. Wasn't it she who had said she would do anything to make her business a success? Just how hard would it be to move into his house for a month? She would have the space she needed and she would be close by the cottage to keep an eye on the renovations. And she did need to go to Paris.

It was a no-brainer, really. But could she really cope with living under the same roof as him? When there was this strange push-and-pull thing going on between them...attraction vying with wariness?

But it wasn't as if he was welcoming her with open arms anyway. He was a busy man who travelled the world. She mightn't see him for most of the time she was his guest.

A little while later, she was about to go about unpacking her car when she glanced around to see him watching her with a dark intensity.

How long would it take for him to regret asking her to stay? If he wasn't already doing so...?

CHAPTER FOUR

MONDAY MORNING. THEY HAD flown to Paris the day before, and today he had a number of client and in-house meetings before him. The acquisition had gone through on Friday evening.

He had set Aideen up with a temporary studio space in the library of the chateau, and she planned on spending the day organising meetings with clients.

He jogged past the walled garden in the grounds of the chateau and then broke into a sprint. He had dined out last night with his French management team. Glad to have an excuse to leave the chateau and her offer to cook them dinner.

They had both worked on the plane over yesterday afternoon, but he had found his gaze repeatedly wandering towards her, intrigued by how absorbed she had been in her work. With her hair swept up into a messy bun she had stared at her laptop screen, her long fingers tapping the delicate column of her neck in thought. And he had wondered what it would be like to have those fingers run against his skin.

After that, the thought of sharing dinner alone with her had set alarm bells off in his brain. He had to keep his distance.

Taking the steps of the garden two at a time, he ran across the stone terrace that traversed the entire length of the back of the sixteenth-century chateau. He entered the house and walked towards the kitchen. Was that *baking* he smelt?

An explosion of household goods were scattered across the surface of the island. The shells of juiced oranges, an upturned egg carton, an open milk bottle teetering precariously on the edge of the unit. Behind them, a trail of baking tins and bowls was scattered along the kitchen counter.

He turned to the sound of footsteps out in the corridor. Aideen walked towards him, a huge bunch of multi-coloured tulips in her arms, a carton of eggs in her hand, rosy-cheeked and bright-eyed, a wide smile on her face. Her hair, thick glossy waves of soft chestnut curls, fell down her back.

'Oh, you're back.' She flashed him a quick smile before her gaze darted guiltily to the chaos behind him. 'I thought you would be out for a while yet.'

'What's happened to the kitchen?'

'I'm making breakfast. I hope you don't mind.'

Actually, he did. He wanted his kitchen clean and tidy, as it usually was. Not this mess.

She sidestepped him and began to search through the kitchen cupboards.

He gritted his teeth and tried to resist the urge to start clearing up the mess himself. His stomach, however, had very different thoughts as it rumbled at the delicious sweet smells of baking.

She plopped the tulips in a vase she had found in a cupboard and placed it on the kitchen table. 'I met your gardener earlier, and he gave me the use of his bike to cycle down to the village so that I could go to the *boulangerie*. But then I ran out of eggs, so I had to go again. The cycle down is easy but, boy, the hill back up is tricky. The countryside here is beautiful, and the village is so pretty. When I came back he gave me these flowers from the garden—aren't they stunning?'

The tulips did look good, but something about their cheery presence in the kitchen niggled him...they were just too *homely*.

For a few seconds she looked at him expectantly. When he didn't respond she smiled at him uncertainly, before rolling up the sleeves of her pink and white striped shirt.

'I'll tidy up here and then put some breakfast on. In honour of being in France, I'm going to make us *oeufs en cocotte*.'

He looked at her, bewildered. And slowly it dawned on him that she was expecting them to have breakfast *together*.

For a few brief seconds he was tempted to give in to the tantalising aroma of fresh baking filling the room. But a glimpse of her white lace bra as she bent over to swoop up the errant milk cap from the floor had him coming back to reality with a bang.

This wasn't what her stay was supposed to be about. A bed and an office... Not seeing too much of her. *That* was what he had signed up for. Not this cosy domesticity. Not some breakfast routine that could quickly become a habit. Not feeling desire for a woman first thing in the morning.

'I don't eat breakfast.'

It was almost the truth. He usually just grabbed some toast and coffee and took it to his office, eager to start work.

She was going about gathering up all the empty packaging on the island unit and paused briefly to give him a quick look. 'But that's crazy. After exercising you should eat.'

His spine stiffened and his jaw muscles tightened. Irritated, he grabbed a mug from the cupboard and went about making himself a coffee. 'I'm not hungry.'

At the sink, she rinsed out a cloth before she turned and caught his gaze. 'Have *something*. I wanted to thank you for having me here. For the flight over…the accommodation. I have some croissants and a baguette I bought in the *boulangerie* earlier warming in the oven.' She stopped and grimaced before admitting, 'My first attempt at *oeufs en cocotte* didn't quite work out, so I had to pop out for more eggs, but I'll have them ready in ten minutes.'

For a moment he almost wavered. 'I appreciate the gesture, but I'll stick to my usual coffee.'

With a disappointed sigh she added, 'If you won't eat, at least let me make the coffee for you.'

He threw his hands up in surrender. 'If you insist—two shots of espresso.'

'I've set the table out in the courtyard. If you would like to go out and sit there I'll bring you out the coffee.'

His head darted to the outdoor dining table in the courtyard. His fine china and cut glass sat on top of a white linen tablecloth. A jug of freshly squeezed orange juice sat next to silver salt and pepper pots. The courtyard was filled with an abundance of springtime flowers and the whole setting looked like a magazine feature on the ultimate romantic breakfast.

'Thanks, but I'll stay in here. I have to leave for work soon.'

At the kitchen table he clicked on to his usual newsfeed, using his tablet. He tried to concentrate on the various market analysts' commentary on his acquisition but she'd switched on the kitchen music system to an upbeat radio breakfast show. The DJs spoke in rapid French, sounding like children who had overdosed on a breakfast of sugary cereal.

And as if that wasn't bad enough she then proceeded to chat away herself, over their manic laughter. 'What a beautiful morning! Going to the *boulangerie* this morning reminded me of the summer I spent here as a student. I had an internship in a design house and I was penniless. I ate baguettes for the entire summer. I used to stare longingly at the patisserie stands, wishing I could afford to buy an éclair or, my favourite, a millefeuille.'

She continued this monologue while fiddling with the coffee machine's controls.

'Do you want some help?'

'No, I'm fine. I'll work it out.'

As she fiddled and twisted Patrick stared at the financial reports, very little detail actually registering. What *was* registering was the round swell of her bottom, the long length of her legs in skinny faded denim. Which only added to his growing annoyance.

Was it because he hadn't been with a woman for more than two years that he sometimes caught himself thinking that she was the most beautiful woman he had ever met? It wasn't just her prettiness, the seductive curves of her long-limbed body. Something shone through in her personality—a happiness, a strength of will that was beguiling.

He almost sighed in relief when she eventually popped a mug of coffee before him.

'Milk or sugar?'

'Neither, thanks.'

Sweet Lord, it was the strongest coffee he had ever tasted.

'I've messed up the coffee, haven't I?'

A crestfallen expression on her face, she waited for his answer.

He leant back in his chair and raised an eyebrow. 'I could probably stand on it.'

She moved to take the mug. 'I'll try again.'

'No!' That poor machine couldn't take it.

She planted her hands firmly on her hips. 'I take it you're not a morning person?'

'Correct in one. I like good coffee, silence, and preferably a tidy kitchen—not Armageddon.'

For a brief second a mixture of hurt and anger sparked in her eyes before she turned away.

She switched off the radio and then quickly cleared the countertops. She wiped them down and then filled the sink with a gush of steaming water in readiness to wash the used pots and pans piled high next to it.

A small part of him wanted to relent, to give in to his hungry stomach and her chatter. To start off the day in something other than the usual silence. A silence he now realised was somewhat lonely.

But if this was to work he needed to stand firm. Start as they meant to go along. Better to upset her than to give her any unrealistic expectations of what their time together would be like.

'I'm going for a shower.'

She didn't turn around at his call, just nodded her head in acknowledgement. But when he reached the door she said, 'I was only trying to show my thanks, you know.'

She turned from the kitchen counter and stared at him defiantly.

When he didn't speak she reddened a little and crossed her arms. 'I went to a lot of effort.'

He retraced his steps back across the room to where she stood. Her gaze rose up to meet his. 'Firstly, I don't eat breakfast. Secondly, I think we need to have some clear boundaries if this is going to work.'

She gave a tight laugh. 'What on earth do you mean by "boundaries"?'

Her laugh rightly mocked his stuffiness, and although he knew he deserved it he was in no mood to defend himself. 'Aideen, I want to help you in re-establishing your business. Nothing else.'

Her blush deepened, but her hands clenched tight at her sides. 'I was making you breakfast. That's all. What's the big deal?'

'I don't want you getting any ideas.'

She drew herself up to her full height and plopped a hand on her hip. 'Trust me—I won't. A workaholic, taciturn, controlling man is the last thing I'm looking for in my life.'

Workaholic, he would admit. But taciturn and controlling? What on earth was she talking about?

'Right—explain to me how I'm taciturn and controlling?'

'You had the next month of my life all planned out before you even spoke to me the morning after the storm.'

'So? It was the most logical plan. Even you agreed with it.'

'Yes, I agreed with it. But not once did you stop to understand just how difficult it was for me to accept it.'

Baffled, he asked, 'What do you mean?'

'I mean I lost not only my business last year. I also lost my pride and self-respect. Having to accept help from you made me feel like I was failing again.'

'That wasn't my intention.'

'I know. But maybe if you'd stopped and thought about how I might possibly feel—if you'd asked me my opinion—then you might have understood.'

She had a point, but he wasn't going to admit it. So instead he challenged her. 'And taciturn?'

'Do you really need to ask? You have barely spoken to me in the past two days.' Biting her lip, she studied him before she added, 'If you don't want me around why did you invite me to stay with you?'

Her bluntness left him for the first time in his life slightly speechless. But then anger rose up in him. 'I don't *do* breakfast...or small talk. I'm not going to be your friend. Now, if you will excuse me, I have to get ready for work.'

He marched away, down the long corridor and up the stairs to the master bedroom, yanking off his tee shirt as he went. Irritation ate into his bones.

As he stood in the shower he scrubbed his hair and defended himself against what she'd said. He wasn't controlling...or taciturn. She was exaggerating. She was saying he was wrong for being decisive. Well, 'decisive' had got him where he was today.

But as the water pounded down on his scalp the uncomfortable realisation that her words might have some truth began to creep into his consciousness.

Had focusing solely on work for so long numbed him to others' feelings? Yes, he was decisive and logical... but did he sometimes steamroller over others?

And as he dressed he began to grasp why he had been

so disturbed by her attempts to make him breakfast. Why it had irked him so much.

It had unsettled him just how good it was to arrive home to activity, to the comfort of having another person in the house. Of course the fact that it was Aideen, looking so happy and gorgeous, added to that uncomfortable realisation. Because it would be so easy to fall into the trap of enjoying her company, of wanting more with this woman.

Aideen emitted a low groan and dropped her head down on to the smooth mahogany wood of the library desk.

Could this day get any worse? First she had messed up with Patrick at breakfast. What was supposed to have been a small gesture of thanks had blown up in her face. Why hadn't she just let him walk away? Did it really matter that he hadn't wanted to accept her gesture of thanks?

He had left for meetings soon after, with a curt goodbye, and she had spent the day alone in this breathtakingly beautiful chateau, on a hill overlooking the Seine, annoyed about their argument but having to be cheery as she made phone calls to organise her own meetings for the coming days.

Several times with prospective new clients she hadn't even got past the receptionist. But she had eventually managed to organise enough meetings to make the trip worthwhile—some with colleagues she hadn't seen since she'd lost her old business.

Just now she had ended another call to an ex-client. The entire call had been a tense mixture of arduous questioning and awkward silences that had left her feeling completely flustered.

'Tough call?'

Her head jerked up and her stomach lurched as she saw Patrick standing in the doorway.

'The usual.'

She was cross with him—and hurt, and embarrassed. And she couldn't bring herself to look at him. But when he came and sat on the table she was working at she couldn't help but glance in his direction.

'I'm sorry for not being tidy…for taking over the kitchen. I just wanted to say thank you for everything you have done by making you breakfast… I guess it back-fired.'

'You don't need to thank me. I suppose I'm finding it a little strange to be sharing my home with someone else.'

She'd only been here a day and he was regretting it already. She shuffled some books and placed fistfuls of marker pens and pencils into canisters, glad that her hair had fallen forward and blocked his view of her face. Which was burning in embarrassment.

'I can move out, if this isn't working for you.'

The touch of his hand on her arm had her jerking back in surprise. Her stomach flipped and her throat tight-ened when she looked at him, her eyes transfixed by the perfection of his thick dark eyebrows, now drawn into a frown, and by the length of his fingers when he drew a hand over his cheek in a gesture of exasperation.

'No. That's not what I mean. I think we need to give each other space, but also adapt to the other person's way of doing things. I've been under time pressure recently, with the demands of my work. I might have rushed to make decisions without taking how you would feel into consideration.'

She felt stupidly relieved by his words, and without

much thought said teasingly, 'Are you apologising to me in a very roundabout way?'

His lips quirked a fraction. 'I suppose I am.'

'So, basically, I need to stop making a mess of your kitchen and you'll try not to be so grumpy?'

His gaze challenged hers playfully. 'And I'll try to eat some breakfast.'

'You have a deal.'

He pushed himself back a little further along the table, creating more distance between them. 'Now, do you want to talk about that call? Who's Ed?'

Her stomach flipped over. The designer had asked her bluntly why she should use her consultancy over Ed's— her ex. She had put forward her track record in designing, her competitive price points, but she knew the designer was still unconvinced.

As she knew to her cost, Ed could be very persuasive and economical with the truth. There had been little point in protesting that a lot of the designs Ed claimed as his own were in fact hers. The designer wasn't likely to believe her. Of course she could take Ed to the courts as a way to claim her rightful ownership, but she didn't have the financial resources to do so.

And Patrick had heard her conversation.

Embarrassment flamed on her cheeks. She had only told her friends and family some of the details, too hurt and humiliated to tell them everything. So how on earth could she be expected to tell a billionaire that she had been so naïve and trusting? This stunning chateau alone told the story of his incredible success and obvious business acumen.

Also, as stupid as she knew it was, it still hurt that he hadn't wanted her breakfast. And every time she saw him she fancied him even more, which was starting to drive her a little crazy.

She lifted a box on to the table. She couldn't speak. Hurt, attraction, embarrassment all swirled away inside her, turning her brain to mush and catching hold of her tongue.

She worked with her back to him, but Patrick could still see how her fingers trembled as she scattered folders and loose cuts of material on to the desk. It was clear that she was going to pretend not to have heard his question. The surface of the desk was quickly disappearing under a mountain of her belongings.

Who was Ed and what hold did he have over her to cause this unease? Something that felt suspiciously like jealousy twisted in his stomach. He breathed it out. He wasn't going there. This was about helping her professionally. Nothing more. And although he was curious about this he would hold off asking her about him again… for now.

As she fought with the now empty cardboard box a low sigh of exasperation sang from her lips. Strangely compelled to ease her upset, to see her smile again, he stepped towards her and took the box, twisting it flat. A quick glance at the messy desk had him saying, 'This won't do. This room is all wrong. Come with me.'

He grasped her hand in his and almost at a run led her down the corridors of the vast chateau.

'Where are we going?'

'You'll see.'

What on earth was he doing? She should be protesting, should be working. But it felt so good to be chasing down corridors with him, to have his hand holding hers.

He brought her to a vast empty room, bathed in evening sunshine, with the warmth of the sun bouncing off the parquet flooring. White wooden doors and windows formed the entire length of the garden-facing walls.

'This is the orangery, but while you're here you can use it as your studio. The library is too dark and small—especially for someone like you, who likes to...' His mouth lifted ever so slightly and after some thought he said, 'Who likes to spread their work around. This is a better space for you to work in. There are some trestle tables stored in an outside storage room. There's other pieces of furniture stored there, too, that you can use. I can get my staff to move them in here tomorrow morning, when they start work, or if you want we could go and get them now ourselves.'

She was completely thrown, and moved by his suggestion. The room would be perfect to work in. She had two options: thank him and run the risk of the emotion in her chest leaking out in gushing thanks, or brazen it out and tease him back.

It was an easy decision. 'Are you saying I'm messy?'

'Based on the evidence of the papers scattered around the library just now...and the kitchen this morning... then, yes, I'd say pretty confidently that you're messy.'

She gave him a mock withering look. Once again she felt completely disarmed by his thoughtfulness. 'This would be perfect. The light and space in here is incredible. Thank you.'

'Good. Now, how about we go and get those tables?'

A little while later, as he helped to unpack a box, he gestured towards her company's logo.

'Where did you get the idea for your business name? Little Fire?'

'It's what Aideen means in Gaelic.'

'I didn't know that.'

'It also felt like a very apt name for the type of business I want. I want to create a small bespoke design consultancy—to be an innovator in the industry. A consultancy that is respected for its passion.'

'It suits your personality, too.' He said it in a deadpan voice, but once again there was a faint hint of humour sparking in his eyes.

Taken aback, she looked away. When she eventually glanced back the humour was gone.

'Are you going to tell me who Ed is?'

She didn't want to. She wanted to bury him in the past. But she needed to answer his question in some form.

'He was my business partner. I set up the company by myself and he joined me a few years later. I was having cash flow problems and he was able to inject capital into the business. We had been to university together and it felt like a good fit for him to come on board.'

'I'm hearing a big *but* here.'

'A very big "but", unfortunately. He insisted on taking a majority share in the business. After that we expanded too rapidly—spent capital on projects we shouldn't have. I shouldn't have agreed to him having a majority share— it led to an inequality in our partnership and gave him the leeway to overrule me. We started arguing. Eventually it became clear that he wanted me out of the business and he made life difficult for me. I tried hanging in there, but in the end I knew I had to go.'

Perched on a trestle table opposite her, he looked at her sombrely. 'What did he do?'

She pulled a wooden bistro chair to the trestle table she'd been working at and sat. She needed to do something while she spoke to avoid having to look at him. To pretend this was an inconsequential conversation. So she started to order by colour the pile of swatches she would take to her meetings in the coming days.

'He overruled all my decisions. He belittled me in front of clients. He dropped heavy rumours that I was difficult to work with.'

'Is that why you're so hesitant about visiting clients?'

'Yes. It's embarrassing. I don't really know how much he said to our clients and whether they believed him. I'm hoping not… But I'm going to do everything I can to make this a success. I love my job. Adore the creativity involved and all the opportunities I get to work with different designers. No two days are the same. I just have to make sure I build up my client base quickly to meet my overheads.'

She glanced up and caught his eye.

'And you know what? I want to prove Ed wrong, too. He said I would never make it on my own.'

'That's understandable, but be careful that proving him wrong doesn't distract from your energy, from your focus.'

She wasn't quite certain what his point was…and she wasn't sure she wanted to fully understand…so she shrugged it off. 'It won't.'

And he knew she had, because without missing a beat he said, 'Okay, tell me what you're going to do differently with this business.'

It was a good question. She knew instinctively a lot of things she would do differently, but hadn't consciously addressed them. She had been in too much of a rush to start again.

For a few minutes she thought about it, her fingers

flicking against the edges of a blue cotton swatch. What *would* she do differently?

'I need to manage my cash flow better—not expand too quickly. Meet with my clients on a more regular basis...communicate with them.'

He nodded at her answer, but fired another question at her immediately. 'Fine, but at a strategic level what are you going to do differently?'

For a while she was lost as to how to answer him. And then she thought about her client base. 'I need to think through what my target market is... Perhaps I'm too diversified at the moment.'

'Spend time thinking about those issues—those are what matter. Not Ed. Don't waste any more time on him. He's not worth it. You lost that business, which was tough. But it's in the past now. Your focus must be on the future.'

Her pulse raced at his words but she forced herself to smile. 'I know. You're right. I need to go and get some more files from the library.'

She practically ran from the room. She heard him call her name but she didn't turn back. Of course he was right. But the hurt of losing the business lingered stubbornly inside her and it was hard to move on from it. To just push it aside. Everything he said was true and right, but she wasn't ready to hear it yet...especially from a billionaire.

His assistants in Dublin and Berlin had long gone home, but after finishing a conference call with his development team in Shanghai later that evening Patrick checked in with his assistant in Palo Alto. He updated his calendar with her for the coming days and ended the call.

He spent the next hour reading the daily reports he

expected each of the managing directors of his subsidiaries to file.

The projected revenue for a new construction industry project management database was not performing as expected. He emailed the management team responsible and listed the new sales strategy he wanted them to follow.

When that was done he checked the time on his monitor. It was not yet nine. In recent months he had frequently worked until twelve. It felt a little strange to have all this spare time. He switched off the bank of monitors on his desk and walked over to the windows overlooking a dense copse of trees. In the dusk, flocks of birds swirled above the treetops, a pink-tinged sky behind them.

How was Orla doing? Should he call her? One of them would have to end this impasse between them. But it was she who had caused it. It was up to her to call.

From the corner of the window he caught a glimpse of Aideen working in the orangery. She was sitting at a trestle table, staring out towards the garden, lost in thought.

Anger bubbled in his stomach at the treachery of her former business partner. He could understand her desire to prove him wrong. If it was him he would exact revenge. But the guy wasn't worth it. She needed to focus on the future and not on the past.

He was tempted to go and speak to her. What was it about her that drew him to her? He certainly admired her tenacity and her determination to start again. And the moment he was in the same room as her, he was sidetracked by her radiance and beauty. By her positive outlook on life. By her smile. By the thick curtain of hair that seemed to change colour according to the light— chocolate-brown at times, filled with highlights of cinnamon and caramel at other times. By her body, which called to the most elemental parts of him...

Yes, she talked too much, and was way too messy... but after two years of silence part of him yearned for her chatter, for her warmth, for her positive outlook on life.

Another part of him wanted to shut it all out. At least that way he wouldn't be able to mess up a relationship again.

And at times her honesty and openness left him floundering. This morning and this evening she had spoken with an emotional honesty that had made him stop and think. And he wasn't sure if he liked that. She spoke about the past while he preferred to ignore it.

Knowing now, though, what she had gone through with her business collapse, made him want to protect and help her even more. He wanted her business to succeed and he would give her all the support that she required.

He just needed to ensure that he kept it strictly professional.

CHAPTER FIVE

WEARING FOUR-INCH HEELS on a day when she had to race from meeting to meeting using the Paris Métro hadn't been one of her best ideas.

At least her short-sleeved silk button-down dress, which she had designed and created using one of her new range of textiles, was comfortable. And thankfully it had also proved to be a major hit with many of the designers she had met with today. They had commented on the dress the moment she had walked into their studios, and it had been the perfect icebreaker for her to introduce the rest of her range.

Her toes were pinched, though, in her never-before-worn shoes, as she walked out of the headquarters of one of Europe's leading online luxury fashion retailers. But she still didn't regret her refusal to use Patrick's chauffeur for the day.

It was bad enough that they had travelled to Paris on his private jet. That they were staying in his unbelievably beautiful chateau. She couldn't accept any further help from him.

This morning they had travelled together into the centre of Paris and he'd had his chauffeur, Bernard, drop her at her first meeting. She had been too nervous to chat, and for once had been grateful for Patrick's silence.

But as she had been about to leave the car he had looked at her with a gentle kindness that had almost floored her and said, 'Believe in yourself.'

She stepped through the automatic sliding doors out on to the street and paused. The building was at the corner of an intersection of five boulevards. Which way was the Métro again? And would it look odd if she walked barefoot?

And then, a little further down the street, she spotted him—leaning against a lamppost, watching her. She faltered at the intensity of his gaze. And then his mouth curled into a smile and she came to a complete stop. He'd smiled at her. He'd actually *smiled* at her.

She knew she was staring at him in shock but she couldn't help it. He was smiling at her! And it felt like the best thing ever.

She smiled back, beyond caring that she probably looked really goofy. And for a joyous few seconds they simply smiled at each other.

Her heart was beating crazily, and her stomach felt as though it was an express elevator on a busy day.

He was so gorgeous when he smiled. Dressed in a bespoke dark navy suit and a crisp white shirt open at the collar, he wore no tie. Other pedestrians did a double take as they passed him by. And if she'd been in their shoes she, too, would have walked by with her mouth open at the sight of the extraordinarily handsome man standing on the pavement, his eyes an astonishing translucent blue, a smile on his delicious mouth.

Heat rushed through her body, quickly followed by a sharp physical stab of attraction.

As she walked to him she tried to disguise the blush that burnt on her cheeks by fussing with the laptop and samples bags in her hands.

'Hi. What are you doing here?'

'You told me your last meeting of the day was here, so I thought I'd come and see how your day went.'

He said it with such sincerity the air whooshed out of her lungs and she could only stand there, looking at him with a big soppy grin.

This was all so crazy. How on earth had she ended up in the city of love with the most incredible and gorgeous guy in the world smiling down at her?

'You look very happy.'

'I'm working on not being taciturn.'

She had to swallow a laugh as she eyed him suspiciously. 'Are you mocking me?'

'Possibly. How does a martini sound?'

She should say no. Pretend to have some work she needed to do back in his chateau. Keep her distance.

But instead she said, 'That sounds like heaven.'

He signalled down the boulevard. Within seconds a dark saloon had pulled up beside them.

His chauffeur had dropped them at his favourite bar in Paris. It had been a while since he had been to the sleek hotel opposite the Jardin du Luxembourg, but it was still as fun and lively as he remembered. And it served the best martinis in the city.

They had spoken little during the journey. The minute she had sat in the car she had slipped off her shoes, leant her head back on the headrest with a sigh and looked out at the familiar Parisian sights as Bernard took them down the Champs-élysées, then Place de la Concorde, and crossed the river at Pont de la Concorde.

'Are your feet still hurting?'

She had looked at him warily. 'Kind of.' Then, with a rueful smile, she'd added, 'Okay—I admit they're killing me. Lord, I miss my old shoes. Stupid flood.'

When she had earlier refused to use his car for the day, at first he'd been irritated at her stubbornness, but then he'd had to admit to himself a grudging admiration for her determination to be independent. But it did still irk him a little. Using his car would have been no big deal.

The lighting in the bar was low, and light jazz music played in the background. Her eyes lit up when the waiter placed their drinks on the table with a flourish. A kick of awareness at just how beautiful, how sexy she was, caught him with a left hook again.

Earlier that left hook had caught him right in the solar plexus when she had walked out on to the street from her meeting. Her black dress with its splatters of blue-and-cream print stopped at mid-thigh. And long, long legs ended in the sexiest pair of red shoes he'd ever seen. Red shoes that matched the red gloss on her lips. Lips he wanted to kiss clean, jealous of the effect they would have on any other man.

Despite himself he hadn't been able to stop smiling at her. And when she'd smiled back, for the first time in a long time, life had felt good.

'So, how was *your* day?'

It had been so long since anyone had asked him that question he was taken aback for a few seconds. She leant further across the table and looked at him expectantly, with genuine interest. Tightness gripped his chest. He had pushed so many people away in the past two years. And

now this warm, funny and vibrant woman made him realise two things: how alone he had been and how much
he must have hurt those he had pushed away.

Would the same thing happen to her?

He felt as though he was being pulled by two oppos-
ing forces: the need to connect with her versus the guilt
of knowing that by doing so he was increasing the likelihood of hurting her when it was time for her to return
to her cottage.

But once again the need to connect won out.

'It went well. I finalised my negotiations to buy out
a mobile software application for hospital consultants.'

'That's brilliant. Congratulations.'

She lifted her martini glass and together they toasted
the negotiations. It felt good to celebrate an acquisition
with someone after all this time.

Her head tilted in curiosity. 'What are you smiling
about?'

He scratched his neck and looked at her doubtfully.
Oh, what the heck? He would tell her. 'I was just thinking that sitting in a bar with you, toasting an acquisition,
sure beats my attempts to train the dogs to high-five my
acquisitions.'

Her laughter was infectious, and they both sat and
grinned at each other for a long while.

'You can always pop down to my cottage to celebrate
in future.'

Instantly a bittersweet sadness reverberated in the air
between them. Across the table her smile faded, and he
could see her own doubt as to whether they could ever
have such an easy relationship.

He needed to get this conversation back on neutral
ground. 'Tell me about your day.'

She gave a groan. 'My first meeting was a disaster. It was with an ex-client who grilled me on the stability of my business and how I was going to deliver on projects now that I didn't have a team behind me.'

Her hand played with her glass and her chest rose heavily as she exhaled.

'To be honest, after that meeting I was ready to give up and head home.' A smile formed on her mouth. 'But on the Métro I thought about what you said to me this morning—to believe in myself.' She paused and ducked her head for a moment. When she looked up, there was a blush on her cheeks, but resolve fired in her eyes. 'I decided you were right. So I dusted myself down and got on with the next meeting.'

This morning she had been visibly nervous about her meetings, but he had deliberately not asked too many questions, nor overwhelmed her with his ideas on how she should approach things. He knew he needed to give her some space. Allow her to face this on her own.

Her comments about him being controlling had hit home and he was consciously trying to curtail his perhaps, at times, overzealous attempts to help her. He would help—but at the pace she needed. That hadn't stopped him from thinking about her all day. Or from leaving his meeting in the eighteenth arrondissement early to ensure he was there when she left her last meeting.

'The rest of the day went much better, thankfully. At lunchtime I met up with a designer friend, Nadine, who is over here from London on business, too. She has just received a major order from a chain of exclusive US boutiques—it will completely transform her business. And she wants me involved, which is really exciting.'

She smiled with such enthusiasm he was sorely tempted to lean across and kiss those full, happy lips.

She scanned the room and gave a nod of approval. 'Great choice of bar, by the way.'

He had to lean towards her to be heard properly above the chatter and music surrounding them. 'I used to live in St Germain before I moved to the chateau.'

'You *lived* in St Germain! I've always dreamt of living in the centre of Paris. Oh, you were so lucky. No offence—your chateau is lovely and everything—but why did you move?'

He wasn't sure he liked the direction this conversation was going in, so he gave a noncommittal answer. 'I like the space and peace of the chateau.'

A shake of her head told him she wasn't going to let it go. 'But you have that already, with Ashbrooke. Why would you want to live outside Paris when you have this incredible city to explore?'

He took a sip of his martini. 'I was tired of city life. And, like at Ashbrooke, I wanted peace and quietness in which to focus on my work.'

She shook her head in bewilderment before saying, 'Just for me, describe your apartment here.'

He was about to say no, but she looked at him so keenly, so hungry for detail, that despite his better judgement he gave her a brief outline. 'It was a two-storey penthouse in a Haussmann building overlooking Île de la Cité.'

'So you had views of Notre-Dame and Sainte-Chapelle? Remind me again why you gave *that* up.'

'For the peace of the countryside—for the space.'

'But why do you have all that space if you have no one to share it with?'

Taken aback by the bluntness of her question, and because it was too close to the bone, he speared her with a look. 'You really don't hold back, do you?'

Her head tilted for a moment and then she said in a more conciliatory voice, 'Not really... But why do you live in such isolated spots? What's the attraction?'

'I spent most of my twenties travelling the world to meet work demands. In recent years I've wanted more stability, a less chaotic and frantic pace. So I've opted to work out of Ashbrooke predominantly and travel only when necessary. And, anyway, I like the countryside. Who *wouldn't* want the ocean views that are at Ashbrooke?'

'I love the countryside, too... But you live behind tall walls, away from the rest of the surrounding communities. Do you never feel alone?'

Lord, she was like a dog with a bone. With someone else he would have cut them off a long time ago, but she asked these questions with such genuine curiosity he found himself reluctantly answering them.

'I don't have time to even *think* of being alone, never mind feel it. Trust me—it's not an issue in my life.'

'What about friends and family? Do you see them often?'

Right—he'd had enough of this. Time to change the subject. 'I see them occasionally.' He nodded at their now empty glasses and said, 'Would you like to walk in the Jardin du Luxembourg before we head back home?'

She nodded enthusiastically, and as they walked out of the bar together his attention was hijacked by the sensual sway of her hips in the high heels. Bewildered, he shook his head, trying to figure out just what was so hypnotic about her walk—and also how she'd managed to get him to talk about personal issues he had never discussed with a single other person before.

The martini and the relief of having survived the hurdle of visiting clients for the first time had combined to make her a little light-headed. So she had happily accepted his suggestion that they stroll through the park.

The paths were busy with joggers and families. A few times she caught Patrick smiling at the antics of careening toddlers and something pulled tight in her chest.

Did he ever want a family of his own? The question was on the tip of her tongue a number of times but she didn't dare ask.

They passed by a bandstand, where a brass band played happy, toe-tapping tunes to a smiling and swaying audience.

'I spoke to William today. The renovations are going well. You'll be glad to hear I will be out of your hair in less than a month after all. It might be three weeks, tops.'

He glanced across at her and then away. 'That's good news.'

A dart of disappointment had her asking, 'That I'll be gone soon?'

He came to a stop and folded his arms. He looked down with good-humoured sternness. 'No. That the renovations are going well.'

Emotion swirled in her chest. She shuffled her feet on the gravel path and she, too, crossed her arms. 'I'm really grateful for everything you have done.'

He looked beyond her, towards a group of children sailing model wooden sailboats on a pond. 'It's not a big deal.'

Of course it was a big deal. But he clearly didn't want to make out that it was.

Evening stubble lined his jaw, adding a rugged masculinity to his already breathtaking looks. How incredible it would be to feel free to run a hand against that razor-sharp jawline and to look into the eyes of this strong, honourable man. Her heart hammered at the thought that in the future some other woman might get close enough to him, might feel free to do exactly that. And he might welcome it.

She pushed away the jealousy that twisted in her stomach. Instead she nodded towards the children he was looking at and said, 'My dad's hobby is model boats. As a child I spent a lot of my Sundays standing in the freezing cold in Herbert Park in Dublin, wishing his boat would sink so that I could go home.'

He gave a bark of laughter and shook his head. 'You sound like you were a wicked child.'

'I used to get into a fair share of trouble, all right. I always blamed my two older brothers, though! Did Orla do that with you?'

He gave a heavy sigh. 'Don't get me started. She used to insist on coming everywhere with myself and my friends. Half the time she would cause mischief—running through people's gardens as a shortcut, helping herself to something from their fruit trees along the way. But when neighbours rang to complain it was always me they mentioned, never Orla. She was so small they couldn't see her.'

For the first time since they'd met he was speaking with genuine ease and affection about someone close to him. He was so animated and relaxed she longed for it to continue for a while.

'What was the village you grew up in like?'

'Everyone knew everyone. I went to the local school and spent my weekends with my friends—either on the beach or playing at our local Gaelic football club.'

Referring to the two traditional Gaelic sports played in most clubs, she asked, 'Hurling or football?'

'Both, of course.' For a while he paused, and then he said, 'I still remember my first day going to the club. My mum took me down and I was so excited to be wearing the club jersey. All the other boys on the street wore it all the time.'

Her chest tightened. 'Do you remember a lot about your mum?'

His voice was sad when he said, 'Just snapshots like that.'

And then he began to walk away.

She had lost him. To that silence he often fell into. She wanted to bring him back.

She followed him and after a while said, 'So, do you get your good looks from her or your dad?'

That elicited a smile. 'So you think I'm good-looking?'

'You know you are. I bet you were the heart-throb in school.'

He laughed at that. 'To answer your question—I take after my dad. Orla's more like my mum.'

'What was your dad like?'

'Hard-working, loving, supportive. A family man and a good neighbour. Orla and I were the centre of his world. He worked several part-time jobs to ensure he was at home when we were. Money was pretty scarce. It used to worry me, but he would just shrug and say that as long as we had one another that was all that mattered. When Mum died he was determined we wouldn't miss out. He even learned how to sew so that he could make us costumes for school plays.'

A lump formed in her throat at hearing the love for his father in his words. In a quiet voice she said, 'He sounds like he was a really good man.'

His eyes met hers for a moment. She felt her breath catch to see the soft gratitude there.

'He was. Each Christmas he would leave us both a memory chest under the tree, filled with little mementos he had collected for us during the year: our sporting medals, awful paintings and poems we'd created in school that only a parent could love, photos of our holidays.'

He paused as a catch formed in his throat. It was a while before he continued.

'In the chests he would also leave a handwritten list with all the reasons why he loved us.'

Her own throat felt pretty tight, but she forced herself to speak. 'What a lovely idea.'

He nodded to that.

They walked beside the urn-lined Medici Fountain and paused where Acis and Galatea, the lovers from Greek mythology, carved in white marble, lay reclined in a lovers' embrace. Their embrace was so intimate she had to look away.

'You said you used to worry about money when you were younger? Is that what motivates you now?' she asked.

'Partially. But it's also the challenge, and knowing that my products are making a difference in people's lives. Especially in the medical field, where they can have a huge impact on how services are delivered to patients. I also like to know that I can provide for others, too.'

She wondered if he meant Orla, but something in the look on his face kept her from asking.

They continued walking, and she said after a while, 'I'm sorry you lost your mum and dad…Patrick. It must have been very difficult.'

'You just get on with it, don't you? There's no other choice.'

'How old were you when you lost them?'

He inhaled deeply before he spoke. 'Seven with my mum…twenty-two with my dad.'

He'd been so young. To lose your mum at seven… She couldn't even begin to think about losing her parents, never mind at that age. 'What age was Orla?'

'She was just a baby with my mum—sixteen when my dad died.'

'Oh, the poor thing.'

He glanced towards her, and then away again quickly, but not before she saw the pain in his eyes. 'Orla found my dad when she came home from school one day. He had died from an abdominal aneurysm.'

For a while she was lost for words. What could she say about such a terrible loss? 'I'm so sorry. It must have been a terrible shock for you both.'

'It was.'

'I bet you were a great older brother, though, which must have helped her a lot.'

Instantly he stiffened and a coolness entered his voice. 'I tried to be.' He gave his watch a quick glance. 'We'd better get back. I have a conference call with Palo Alto in less than an hour.'

Thrown by the sudden change in conversation, and knowing instinctively that he deliberately wanted to end their chat, she looked at her mobile phone. It was almost eight.

'Do you have to take that call? You never seem to stop working.'

He gave a quick shrug. 'I have a problem with a system roll-out over there.'

'But you must have endless directors. Do you really need to have such a hands-on role?'

They exited the park and walked towards Bernard, who was waiting at the kerb.

Patrick answered. 'I like to be involved.'

As they approached the car she said, 'More like you like being in control.'

He looked at her unhappily. 'It's not that simple.'

About to slip into the car, she asked, 'Are you sure?'

He sat beside her and his rigid jaw and thinned mouth told her he was in no way happy with her comment.

He turned and fixed her with a lancing stare. 'It's my *responsibility* to be in control. I will not let down those who are dependent on me—in the workplace or otherwise. I will not apologise to anyone for doing my job.'

She was taken aback by the cold fury in his voice, but he had his mobile out and was speaking rapidly to someone before she could even respond.

CHAPTER SIX

A SET OF preliminary moss-green and off-white designs stared back at her from the laptop screen, as though willing her to make a decision.

Ever since Patrick had asked her what she was going to do differently with her business the question had constantly played on her mind. Time and time again she came back to the one major decision she had to make. Would she stop designing for the upholstery market in favour of specialising exclusively in fashion textile design—her true love?

And now she had to decide whether to submit these designs to Dlexa, a world-renowned upholstery textile manufacturer. Would she be crazy *not* to? It was a huge gamble to take. The upholstery business had often seen her through lean times. But it was also a distraction that ate into time she could be devoting to the fashion market.

So many times during the past few days she had been tempted to go and talk it through with Patrick, to get his advice. So much for her resolve to do this on her own...

Not that she had seen enough of him during the past few days to have such a conversation anyway. Their paths seldom crossed...and she had a sneaking suspicion that he had engineered it that way. Yes, they were both working incredibly long hours. And he was either out at meetings or locked away in his office at the chateau. Once or twice he had appeared in the kitchen while she was preparing a meal. But he'd always had an excuse to leave—something needing his attention elsewhere.

She tried not to let it get to her. Tried not to dwell on the fact that it was probably because she had said too much the other night. Asked too many questions. Tried to get to know him a little better.

At times she'd got a glimpse of a different man from the work-obsessed CEO the world saw. But as quickly as he opened up that fun and playful side he would shut it down again.

What did she expect, anyway? The man ran countless multimillion-pound companies. He wasn't going to have time to chat to her over a coffee.

She constantly felt as though she was waiting for him to appear, with a low-lying nervous anticipation she couldn't dispel. Each night disappointment sat heavily in her chest as she walked to her bedroom, knowing that yet another day had gone by without her seeing him for more than a few minutes. And in the mornings that disappointment was transformed into equally inexplicable excitement at the prospect of seeing him.

The designs for Dlexa would take at least another twenty to thirty hours of work to complete. Would it be worth the investment of her time? Her gut was telling her to specialise, to follow her dreams. But flashing in neon lights in her mind's eye was the total sum in her bank account, which had made her blanch when she'd checked it earlier today.

She needed a coffee.

His housekeeping staff had left for the day, leaving

behind, along the chateau's corridors, the smell of bees-wax and the air of contentment that settled on a newly cleaned and polished space.

In the kitchen she tackled the beast of a coffee machine. It still made her nervous. There were way too many knobs and buttons for her liking. But she was slowly getting the hang of it and its temperamental nature. Thankfully so, because it produced the best coffee she had ever tasted.

She was about to head back to the studio when she spotted a parcel on the kitchen table, wrapped in luxurious cream paper and thick gold ribbon. The card on top was addressed to her.

Intrigued, she opened the card.

Aideen,
We are sorry the sea ate your shoes. We gathered
all our treat money together to buy you a new pair.
Love, Mustard and Mayo
PS: We promise not to chew them when you return
to Ashbrooke. We hope you are enjoying Paris.

Inside the parcel, wrapped in individual silk pouches, she found the most exquisite ivory ankle-strap sandals. High enough to make her feel a million dollars, low enough for her to actually be able to walk in them.

They were stunning; if she had seen them in a store she would have fallen over herself to hold them just for a little while. But she couldn't accept them. Her pride had already taken a severe dent at the amount of help she'd had to accept from Patrick. It was humiliating to take so much and give so little in return.

And, given his remoteness in recent days, she didn't even understand why he was giving them to her.

She needed to go and speak to him—figure out why he was giving them to her and then somehow explain why she couldn't accept the gift.

She knocked and waited at the partially open door of his office. He opened the door with a phone to his ear and gestured for her to come inside.

He sat down behind his desk, his eyes moving speculatively to the package in her hand.

Her belly tightened and she turned away, inspecting the modern paintings hanging on the French Grey walls, failing to convince herself that his deep, authoritative and decisive voice had no effect on her. She tried not to listen to his conversation but was intrigued by the way he was able to quickly fire out the pros and cons of purchasing an office block in Rio de Janeiro. He ended the call with an order to proceed with the sale.

Her chest swelled with admiration. She wanted to be like that. Certain and unwavering in her decision-making.

His office was incredibly neat. The desk contained four different monitors, a keyboard, a ream of paperwork neatly stacked into a pile and nothing else. No empty cups, pens askew, or sticky notes scattered with random thoughts like on her own desk. No wonder he thought her messy. The guy was a perfectionist. Perhaps, to achieve what he had, he'd had to be.

'Take a seat.' He gestured over to two silver-green velvet-upholstered sofas that sat before the fireplace. He replaced the handset in its cradle before he moved over to sit on one himself.

She sat, and placed the parcel on her lap. For a moment she stared down at it, the shoe-lover in her reluctant to give it up. But then she placed it on the coffee table between them and pushed it towards him.

'Thank you for the shoes but I can't accept them.'

To that he simply raised an eyebrow.

A knot of tension grew in her belly.

'Giving me accommodation and a place to work for a month, flying me to Paris... You've been more than generous. I can't accept anything else from you—it wouldn't be right.'

'They're just a token from Mustard and Mayo.'

She couldn't help but say in amusement, 'Dogs who internet-shop? Now, *that's* clever.'

For a moment he looked as if he was going to insist, but then he leant towards her. 'Why don't you tell me why you can't accept them?' When she smiled, he held his hands up in admission and said, 'See? I *do* listen to you. This time I'm going to try and understand why before I try to persuade you otherwise.'

'It's not that I don't like them...they're beautiful...or that I'm not grateful.' She came to a stop and her heart was beating so wildly she felt light-headed.

She bent her head and inhaled deeply, clasping her hands. She squeezed her fingers extra-hard.

'I think I should explain...'

Was she crazy, telling him this? But she wanted him to know. So that he would stop ruining all her plans to be independent by giving her so much.

She glanced at him quickly, and then looked away from his frown and stared out of his office window, seeing the tips of the trees blowing in the light breeze.

'After I lost my business I swore I would never be dependent on or beholden to another person again.'

'What do you mean by "beholden"?' His tone was sharp.

She struggled to find the right words to explain what she meant. 'I mean...not indebted to another person. I don't want to feel that I always have to be grateful—that I owe someone else. That I have no right to voice my opinions. But it's not just that... I have to prove to myself that I'm not a failure. And accepting all your help feels like I'm cheating, somehow.'

He looked taken aback, and then he argued, 'You're not a failure if a business deal goes wrong. It happens to a lot of people. At least you had the guts to risk everything in creating a business in the first place. Not everyone could do that. And accepting the help of a neighbour is not cheating.'

He stood and paced the room, his jaw working.

'And I certainly will never—and I mean *never*—make you feel obliged or indebted. I am not that type of person.'

She flinched at the annoyance in his voice. She was making a mess of this. She needed to tell him everything. Then maybe he would understand.

'I'm trying to be honest with you. I want you to understand and I'm sorry if I'm offending you. Let me try and explain...then you might understand. My business partner...Ed. He was my boyfriend, too.'

Heat rose in her cheeks and she stopped as humiliation gripped her throat. She bit the inside of her cheek.

'Not only did he manoeuvre it so that I had no option but to walk away from the business, but he was also having an affair with our finance director.'

She jumped when she heard him utter a low expletive, and was taken aback by the dark anger that flared in his eyes.

'What an idiot.'

'I know. Him…and me.'

'No! The guy's despicable. Don't for one second think you were in anyway responsible.'

'But that's the problem. I was. I shouldn't have agreed to him owning a higher percentage share in the business. I shouldn't have believed all the lies he told me. I honestly can't believe I was so stupid. That's what I hate most— I'm now so wary of others. It's one of the reasons why I can't even accept the shoes. It's not just that they're way too expensive, but I keep wondering *why* you're being so kind and generous.'

He stopped pacing and looked at her with breath-stealing intensity. 'Because just maybe we are not all jerks. Some of us might actually have a heart and want to do the right thing.'

'I'm finding that hard to believe.'

'Don't let him have the power to change you, to make you unhappy.'

'I know… In my heart I know all that. But I can't stop these feelings.'

Across from her he folded his arms on his chest. A look of frustration joined his anger. 'You don't trust me, do you?'

Completely taken aback she gabbled nonsensically. 'No! Yes…I'm not sure… We don't really know one another. Oh, God, I'm sounding really rude. I didn't come here to insult you, and I'm sorry if I have. I just want you to understand why I can't accept anything else from you. It's not that I'm not grateful…call it pride, self-respect… I just can't. I hope you can understand?'

With a raised eyebrow and a quick shrug he said, 'I'm trying to.'

Part of her wanted to turn and run. This conversation had not been a success by any stretch of the imagination. She had insulted him and annoyed him and possibly even hurt him. She needed to try to make amends. Starting with showing some trust in him.

She inhaled a deep breath and began to talk. 'I'm sorry. I honestly didn't come here to insult you. I wanted to explain about the shoes. But I also came in the hope of some advice.'

His brow had creased with doubt but she forced herself not to stop.

'I'll keep it short. You said I should think about my business strategy. Well, there's an area of my business that brings guaranteed revenue, but it's time-intensive work and it's in an area I don't particularly want to specialise in. I'm thinking of not submitting work in that area again, but I'm worried about the revenue.'

'What's the worst-case scenario?'

'I lose revenue for a few months.'

With a quick nod he fired another question at her. 'Can you absorb that loss?'

'Just about.'

'And if the drop in revenue continues for longer?'

'I can always re-enter that market… It will take time to build my portfolio back up, but it's doable.'

He didn't ask any more questions, but instead walked back to his desk. After a while she realised he was waiting for her to speak. And she also realised she had her answer.

With a light shrug, she smiled. 'I think I know what I should do.'

He nodded. 'I think you do.'

As she went to leave the room he called after her.

'Are you certain about the shoes?'

Her hand on the door, she paused, and it was a while before she could turn around. After all she had said he was still being kind. But maybe he was also indirectly asking if she still didn't trust him.

Her heart turning over, she faced him. 'Maybe some time in the future?'

His eyes narrowed at that, and she fled down the corridor before either of them had a chance to say anything further.

Standing at his office window later that evening, Patrick spoke to his chief financial officer while staring out at yet another incredible dusk sky. This evening it was a riot of pink, lilac and lavender, with faint wisps of cloud to the forefront.

A movement on the terrace caught his attention. Aideen was out there, photographing the sunset. Wearing jeans and a silver and grey top, she had her hair pulled back into a high ponytail, exposing the delicate angles of her face, her full lips, the smooth jawline and long, slim neck.

Too distracted to concentrate, he ended the call early and stood watching her.

Their earlier conversation had been difficult. The shoes had been his way of saying he was sorry about everything she had lost in the flood…and for being so tetchy in recent days.

After their walk in the park the other night he had opted to keep his distance from her. He had revealed too much of himself. And he didn't like how good it had felt to be in her company. Her comment about being a good brother to Orla had only reminded him of how he had failed, and of all the reasons why he needed to keep his distance from Aideen.

But the shoes had unwittingly hit a raw nerve with her.

He cursed out loud when he remembered the raw pain etched on her face when she had described her ex's betrayal. No wonder she was slow to trust him. Not that it hadn't stung to hear her admit it.

But knowing what she had gone through strengthened his resolve that nothing could happen between them. He had to suppress his attraction to her. She had just come out of a destructive relationship. The last thing she needed was to be hurt again. And a messy relationship with him was a sure way for her to get hurt.

She needed practical support right now—not a lover. Not all the complications and misunderstandings and raw emotions and intimacy that went with that.

He opened the door from his office out on to the terrace and walked to where she was now sitting, on a wooden bench on the first tier of the terraced garden. The grass muffled his footsteps and when he called her name she looked up in surprise.

'I saw you taking some photos.'

Angling the camera towards him, she asked, 'Would you like to see them?'

He sat beside her and watched the images as she flicked through them on the viewfinder.

'They're beautiful. Will you use them in your work?'

'Probably. They will look great in silk.'

As she kept on flicking the pictures of the sky disappeared and a family portrait appeared in the viewfinder.

With a fond laugh she said, 'Welcome to my family.' She zoomed in closer. 'That's my mum and dad. My brother Fionn.' Then she flicked through another few photos until she found a close-up of a family of three. 'And this is my brother Gavin and his wife Tara, with their little girl, Milly.'

In the photo Gavin and Tara gazed down at their baby with utter devotion. Something kicked solidly against his gut. And kicked even harder when Aideen flicked on to a close-up of Milly.

'Isn't she so beautiful? I never realised just how much I would fall in love with her. The day Gavin rang to say she had been born…' She paused and shook her head in wonder. 'I honestly have never been so happy. You might even have heard my screams of excitement all the way up in Ashbrooke!'

Aideen's enthusiasm and love for Milly slammed home just what he was going to miss. He was never going to get to know Orla's baby. He coughed as a sharp pain pierced his heart.

She looked at him in concern and said, 'Are you okay?'

What was it about her that made him want to tell her? Was it that he was tired of holding in all the hurt and anger inside himself? Was it that she was so open herself?

'My sister Orla is expecting a baby. Next month, in fact.'

Her mouth dropped open in surprise. 'Really? That's fantastic. You must be so excited. Oh, wait until it's born. It really is the best feeling in the world. You wi—'

He cut across her. 'It's not that straightforward.'

'What do you mean?'

'Orla and I haven't been getting on.'

'Oh, listen—I argue with my brothers all the time. You'll be fine.'

Her exuberance and happiness were too much. How could he explain to her just how bad things were between him and Orla? How he had failed her? How she didn't trust in him? How she threw everything he did for her back in his face? It was easier to pretend that she was right.

He answered without looking at her. 'Perhaps.'

'Have you bought anything for the baby yet? I went on a crazy spurge before Milly was born. I bought her the most exquisite hand-knitted blanket in a shop in Mooncoyne. You could buy Orla's baby one, too.'

'I transfer money to Orla every month. She can buy whatever she needs.'

She swung forward on the bench to catch his eyes, horror in her own. 'Please tell me you're joking. You're Orla's only family. You *have* to buy her a present.'

He gave her blistering look. 'Now who's being dictatorial?'

She backed off, hands raised. 'Okay. Fair enough.' She paused for a whole five seconds. 'But still—you have to buy something for your... Is it a boy or a girl?'

Frustration ate into his stomach at her question. He didn't know, and it was humiliating and painful all at once. 'I don't know.'

'Oh. Does Orla know?'

He had no idea. To avoid answering her he looked at his watch. 'I have some calls to make.'

As he stood up she said with concern, 'It's gone eight thirty at night—do you really have to make calls now?'

He simply nodded, indicating that he did, but as he went to move away her hand reached out and stalled him.

'Will you just wait for a minute? There's something I want to say to you.'

He was about to argue, but there was a warmth to her eyes that had him sitting down beside her again.

He looked at her suspiciously and she knew she just had to come out and say what was on her mind. 'Can I be a nag for a few minutes?'

He asked warily, 'Can I stop you?'

'The crazy hours you work…'

Something shuttered in his eyes and tension grew in his jawline.

For a moment she was about to apologise for overstepping the mark, but she stopped herself in time. Maybe he needed to hear some of this.

'I know I annoyed you the other night, when I said you just wanted to be in control of everything. It wasn't a fair comment. I understand you have a lot of responsibilities, and I admire how hard you work and everything you have achieved. What I was trying to say was that I reckon you really need more of a balance in your life.'

He crossed his arms on his chest. 'Pot…kettle…black.'

He had a point, but that wasn't going to stop her. 'You're right. We both need to get a life. Stop working such crazy hours and start having a bit more fun.'

His jaw worked and he fixed her with a cool gaze. 'I have a life. One that I'm happy with.'

'But your life revolves around just work. You *must* need downtime. A way of relaxing, blowing off steam. Answer me this—have you dated recently?'

His answer was curt. 'No, I've been too busy with work.'

She rose a sceptical eyebrow.

'What about friends and family? Do you get time to see them?'

'Occasionally.'

'So basically your life is just work? That can't continue. You seem to be very hands-on with all your different subsidiaries—perhaps you should delegate more? That would free up your time and allow you to have a better balance. Time you could spend with those close to you.'

'Are you trying to tell me *again* how to run my businesses?'

His voice was ice-cold, and it stung to be on the receiving end of his displeasure. Who was she, anyway, to tell a successful billionaire that he needed more in his life?

It would be so easy to change the topic. But she was the only person in his life right now, and someone needed to say these things. And she cared for him—possibly more than she should.

Her heart thumped in her chest at his obvious irritation but she ploughed on. 'No, I'm not telling you. I'm just suggesting. Look, I know that you are super-successful, and that I lost my business last year, but that doesn't mean I can't have an opinion. I admit I might be wrong, but at least give it some thought.'

His gaze, rather astonishingly, slowly turned from furious to quizzical to mild amusement. 'I have to give it to you, Aideen. You're pretty tough underneath all that beauty and happiness. I have managing directors of multinational companies who would probably agree with you but wouldn't have the nerve to say so.'

She threw her eyes heavenwards, trying to ignore the pulse of pleasure his words evoked, telling herself he was only joking. 'Well, I can't see how pretending it's otherwise will help you.'

'You think I need *help*?'

He sounded incredulous. What did he think? That he was the only one who could help others? That he was the only one capable of being a knight in shining armour?

'You say you're happy, but my guess is that you could be happier…God knows, I know I could be.'

He looked at her quizzically. 'What do you mean?'

How could she tell him that she was sometimes lonely…sometimes scared about facing life on her own? It would sound so needy. And it would probably set off all types of alarm bells in his brain.

So instead she leant back into the bench and said, 'I miss being spontaneous—living life for the moment. I have been so bogged down in my business for the past five years I think I've stopped knowing how to have fun.'

Giddy relief ran through her body when he gave her a rueful smile. 'Spontaneity? I haven't had a lot of that in my life in a while.'

Something in his smile freed her. 'Let's do something *now*!'

'It's getting late…'

She laughed at the incredulous look on his face. 'Let's go clubbing.'

'I don't think there are many clubs in the village,' he pointed out with a laugh.

'We could go into Paris.'

'Yes, but I have calls I need to make…I won't be finished before midnight.'

'Cancel them.'

'I can't.'

She folded her arms primly and said, 'I told you that you don't know how to have fun.'

For a while he considered her with a smile. But in the

silence a tense awareness blossomed between them. His smile faded and darkness entered his eyes. He leant closer and her heart began to thunder again. She looked up into his eyes, barely able to breathe. He came even closer and his whole body seemed to eclipse hers.

His head slowed, moved down towards hers, and when his mouth was level with her ear he whispered in a lilting, sexy voice, 'You want spontaneity…?'

A deep shiver of desire ran through her. Every pulse-point in her body felt as though it was thudding against her skin. Her body swayed closer to him, desperate to feel his strength and warmth.

Her throat had closed over. She barely managed to whisper, 'Yes…'

His hand lay against her cheek and with gentle pressure he turned her mouth towards his. Their mouths aligned and almost touched. She closed her eyes, suddenly dizzy with wonder. She squeezed her hands into tight balls. She couldn't touch him. Because if she did she was worried she would never be able to let go.

And then his lips were on hers and her entire body turned to jelly. His warm, firm lips teased hers with butterfly kisses and she gave a little sigh. He deepened the kiss. Her arms of their own volition snaked up to grasp the material of his sweater. Beneath her fingers his chest was hard and uncompromisingly male.

Her head swam. She swayed against him. His hard body was like a magnet. She longed to touch every part of him. She wanted more.

When he eventually released his hold on her and pulled away she looked at him, dazed, her senses overloaded.

With a lazy, sexy grin he asked, 'How's that for spontaneity?'

Without thinking, she breathed out in a husky whisper, 'Pretty spectacular, really.'

Her already flushed skin flamed at his obvious amusement at her answer.

Flustered, she added, 'And enough spontaneity for one night, I reckon. I think it's time I went inside.'

She got up to leave, but he placed a hand on her arm. His eyes were soft pools of kind amusement.

'Thank you for tonight...' For a moment he looked down, a hand rising to rub the base of his neck. When he looked up again he said with wry amusement, 'Thank you for the life coaching... You can pop the bill in the post.' And then, with his eyes sparkling, he added, 'And thank you for the kiss.'

It had been the most incredible kiss of her life. But this thing between them was going nowhere.

She gave what she hoped appeared to be a casual shrug, said, 'Goodnight!' and hightailed it up the steps to the terrace.

She walked briskly—first to the orangery, to return her camera, and then to her bedroom with a confusing mix of elation and worry.

It had been the most incredible, tender and emotional kiss she had ever experienced. But neighbours didn't kiss like that...and certainly not with such underlying passion and poignancy.

She lay awake for hours later, their kiss swirling in her brain.

They were only supposed to be neighbours—nothing more.

But they already knew more about each other than many close friends did. She had revealed more about herself than she'd ever done before. And slowly, bit by bit, he was confiding in her.

And, even though she knew they had no future, time and time again her brain wandered off topic and she dreamt of him kissing her. And of that kiss leading to a lot more…

CHAPTER SEVEN

DESPITE BEING ON a teleconference with his Northern Europe management team Patrick found himself zoning out of the conversation about a project delay and losing himself in memories of how good it had been to kiss Aideen last night. The soft fullness of her lips, the press of her breast against his biceps, the low purr of frustration when he had forced himself to pull away...

It had been a stupid and reckless kiss...but a large part of him didn't care. How could he regret something that had felt so good?

But how was he going to play it with her now? In truth, he wanted to throw caution to the winds and kiss her again. And possibly even more. But what of all the messy awkwardness that doing so would cause?

A movement at his office door had him looking away from his screen.

Dressed in navy jersey shorts and a white tee shirt, a pair of white trainers on her feet, Aideen smiled at him cheekily and waved two tennis rackets in the air.

Her long legs were toned, as was the rest of her tall, strong but curvy body. She brimmed with fresh vitality and health. She stepped into the room and he was unable to look away. An image of her brown eyes heavy with pleasure, the heat of her mouth last night, popped into his brain.

The sound of someone coughing had him looking back at the screen. Seven pairs of eyes were looking at him speculatively, no doubt wondering what had caught his attention.

He looked at his team, and then back at her.

He shouldn't. He really needed to finish this call.

'Elsa, take over for me.' He looked towards Aideen and raised an eyebrow, challenging her. 'And, Elsa? Please decide and implement whatever strategy you deem appropriate to get the project back on track. Update me only if there are any issues.'

Aideen was right. It was time he had some fun in his life.

He cut the connection on seven even more stunned looking execs and leant back in his chair. 'I was in the middle of a conference call.'

'You've been in this office since six this morning. You know what they say—all work and no play...'

He stood and walked towards her, doing his best not to allow the threatening smile to break on his lips. 'Are you saying I'm dull?'

He took unexpected pleasure from the blush that blossomed on her cheeks.

She swallowed hard before she spoke. 'No. Never, ever dull.' There was a hint of breathlessness in her voice and she blushed even harder.

'So what's with the rackets?'

'Well, as there's a tennis court worthy of Wimbledon sitting unused outside, I thought we should use it.'

He placed his hands in his pockets and looked at her

with playful sternness. 'Is this a not too subtle way of making me "get a life"?'

'You have me rumbled.' She grinned back cheekily. 'So, are you up to the challenge or are you too scared?'

When she put it like that there was no way he was saying no. 'Give me ten minutes.'

As she turned to leave she said, 'I must warn you, though. I was under-thirteen champion at my tennis club.'

He caught up with her out in the corridor. 'So you think you might be able to beat me?'

'I'll certainly try.'

'How do I put this nicely…? You don't have a hope.'

To that she playfully threw back her head in a gesture that said she wasn't going to listen to him and walked away. About to turn the corner, she turned around. 'Nice delegation, by the way.'

'And I did it without even flinching.'

She gave him a wicked grin and turned away.

She was right. He did need to delegate more. He had a talented and ambitious team surrounding him. And he was starting to suspect that he was holding them back by insisting on such centralised decision-making. He needed to empower his subsidiaries more.

He had once. When he had started out he had given them plenty of autonomy. But in the past few years, as the business had exploded in size, he had reigned them in. The truth was as his home life with Orla had become more fraught he had used work as a way of feeling in control, driven by the thinking that if he couldn't support her emotionally he would at least do so financially. By pulling the businesses back under his control he'd felt as though he was achieving something and he'd been able to bury the feelings that went with failure.

But centralised control wasn't sustainable. It had to change. But relinquishing that control wasn't going to be easy.

Two hours later he threw his racket up in the air in elation. Aideen stood at the opposite end of the court wearing a deep scowl.

'That was *not* out.'

'It was out by a mile. I told you I would win.'

'You didn't give me as much as an inch.'

'Like you did *me* any favours!'

She shook her head and stomped down towards the net. 'I didn't realise you were so competitive.'

'Aideen, in comparison to you I reckon I'm almost comatose.'

With a laugh she conceded, 'I hate losing.'

'So I gathered. Come on. I think we could both do with a drink.'

They walked to the kitchen and he prepared them each a large glass of sparkling water mixed with fresh orange juice. They took them out on to the terrace to drink, a light breeze cooling them down.

Across the table from him she stretched her arm in and out a number of times.

'Cramp?'

'I think I might have pulled a muscle on a return volley.'

'You *did* throw yourself about the court.'

At that she gave a sheepish shrug. 'I admit I can get carried away sometimes. I spent my childhood trying to keep up with my two older brothers. I couldn't help but develop a competitive streak.'

'Your competitiveness…hating to lose…was that one of the reasons why losing the business was so hard for you?'

'I guess. Despite my less than tidy ways, I've always pushed myself hard. I suppose my pride did take a dent. It was the first time in my life I failed at anything.'

Her words immediately resonated with him. His business success highlighted just how badly he had messed up with Orla. It made the success seem somewhat hollow when you didn't have someone to share it with.

She flexed her arm again, and said, in a thoughtful almost sad voice, 'I know I have to think about the future and move on. But it's really not that easy to just wipe away the past. To ignore everything that happened. To bury the pain. I can't help but wish that things had turned out differently.'

Something sharp pierced into him and he practically growled out, 'Were you in love with Ed?'

She blinked rapidly and her mouth fell open. Eventually she answered, 'I thought I was.'

A strange sensation of jealousy seeped into his bones and he had the sudden urge to punch something. He had never felt so possessive of a woman in his life. He needed to change the subject quickly—to distract them both.

'Try to forget him—and everything that happened. I appreciate it's hard, but it's vital you focus on the future. Tell me about your dreams, what you personally want to do in the coming years.'

She eyed him with a mixture of surprise and suspicion. But then she shrugged and said, 'Well, that's a big question.' For the longest while she paused, her brows knitted together in concentration. 'Nothing extraordinary, really. I've always wanted to visit St Petersburg. And travel to Dharamsala in India. Where the most incredible mulberry silk is woven. Afternoon tea in Vienna has always sounded like fun. Oh, and I want to learn how to bake a soufflé.'

'A soufflé?'

'They always sink on me—it drives me crazy.'

Curiosity got the better of him and he couldn't help but ask, even though he wasn't certain what answer he wanted. 'And family and relationships?'

She eyed him warily and it was a while before she answered. 'Check back in with me in a few years' time. Right now I'm not exactly in the mood to be in a relationship. All you men have a black mark against your names.'

'All three and a half billion of us?'

'Yes, every single one. Well, apart from my dad and my brothers.' She hesitated, glanced at him briefly, and then said in a rush, 'And possibly you if you continue being such a good neighbour.'

Trying but failing to ignore the reality check her words had caused, he answered drily, 'Glad to hear that.'

'So what about you? What's on *your* list?'

Like her, it wasn't something he had overly thought about. And yet it was a question that filled him with unexpected excitement. 'I want to continue on with the restoration of Ashbrooke. The east wing in particular needs conservation work. And there's an old bathing house on the grounds I want to restore, as well.'

'You really love Ashbrooke, don't you?'

'Yes, I do. I suppose I have a lot of emotional attachment to it because of Lord Balfe. His family owned the estate for generations and it was a huge honour that he was happy to sell it to me. There were several other interested parties, but he chose me. He spends most of his time in the Caribbean now—growing old disgracefully, by all accounts.'

'Do you see him often?'

'Unfortunately, no. Maybe I should buy a business in the Caribbean so I'd have an excuse to go there.'

'Or…an easier solution…you just take a holiday and go and visit him.'

She smiled cheekily at him and he couldn't help but laugh.

For a while they just looked at each other, the warmth and understanding in her eyes causing his heart to thump in his chest. A deep connection reverberated between them.

A slow blush formed on her cheeks and she leant into the table, her fingers drawing down over the grain of the wooden tabletop. 'What else is on your list?' she asked quietly.

His blood thundered in his ears at the strength of the connection he felt with her. He wanted to tell her about Orla and his dreams of them being close once again. But where would he even start to explain the jumbled up, contradictory one hundred and one emotions he felt for his sister?

Instead he said, 'I want to take part in the Isklar Norseman Xtreme Triathlon in Norway.'

'Now, *that* sounds impressive.' Her eyes sparkled with admiration, but the sparkle slowly faded. 'And relationships?'

What would she say if he told her he could never be in a permanent relationship? That he wasn't interested in being in one? That he was no good in relationships?

That he had lost everyone he had ever loved and never wanted to expose himself to that again?

It was easier to be non-committal rather than get into a debate about it. 'Some day, perhaps.'

She moved forward in her chair, a familiar look of determination growing. 'You won't meet anyone if you're stuck in your office twenty-four-seven.' When he didn't respond, she asked bluntly, 'Are you going to sacrifice the rest of your life to work for *ever*? Are you *so* determined not to let other people in?'

He gave a disbelieving laugh. 'I spend my days speaking to people on the phone. I travel. I speak to my staff.'

'Okay, let's call a spade a spade, here. Work conversations and travel don't count. You don't *really* have people in your life—meaningful relationships. And you want it that way. Plus, you've stopped knowing how to have fun.'

Thrown by the uncomfortable truth of her words, he chose to answer only her latter accusations. 'No, I haven't.'

'Prove it.'

'And if I don't?'

'I'll cook dinner for you tonight.'

'Am I supposed to be scared of that prospect?'

'Just imagine the mess I'd make of your kitchen.'

Despite his best efforts he winced. 'Fine. If you want fun, we'll go out tonight. I'll take you to dinner at one of my favourite restaurants.'

'You're on. But I'm paying.'

'No. It's my idea. I'll pay.'

She threw him a stern look. 'I'm sure you appreciate why I would want to pay.'

He breathed out in exasperation. 'I wish you would just accept my help.'

She looked at him with quiet dignity. 'I don't want to feel like a freeloader.'

Something pulled in his chest and he said in a conciliatory voice, 'Let's just go out and enjoy ourselves. By all means you can pay.'

Though she had insisted she would be paying for the meal, the moment she got back to her bedroom, fretting at the likelihood of jaw-dropping décor with matching prices at his favourite restaurant, she checked her online bank account's balance. Thankfully she wasn't yet in the red.

But it turned out that the restaurant was a traditional bistro, located in the back streets of St Germain. The menu proudly announced that it had been established in 1912. She guessed that the décor—Bakelite lights, simple wooden tables and chairs, tiled floors—hadn't changed a whole lot in all that time. It was utterly charming.

After they'd been shown to their seats by the maître d' she continued to look around. 'It's really lovely here.'

'This is one of my favourite restaurants in Paris. The cooking is excellent and the service friendly.'

Yes, and it was also very romantic, with its low lighting and small, intimate tables with a single candle on each. In fact they were surrounded by fellow diners who were totally engrossed in one another.

This was awkward.

She shuffled in her seat and looked away from the amused glance he threw in her direction.

She was saved from further embarrassment by the arrival of their waiter, who brought them a glass of champagne along with their menus.

Holding his glass up towards her, Patrick said, 'Here's to the success of Little Fire.'

Taken aback by the sincerity in his voice, and his support of her cherished dreams, she felt unexpected tears form at the backs of her eyes. She blinked them away rapidly and took a sip of her champagne.

She read the menu with both relief—she could afford the prices—and growing excitement. Every item on the menu was a mouthwatering classic of French cuisine.

'They have Grand Marnier soufflé for dessert—I'm going to *have* to order that.'

'Why don't you order dinner for both of us?'

She looked from him back to the menu and then back at him, taken aback and slightly horrified. 'But I have no idea what you like.'

He shrugged with amusement. 'I don't care.'

Ed would have walked over hot coals rather than allow her to order for him.

'Are you sure?'

He watched her with an assuredness and yet an intimacy that had her looking back down at the menu with a ricocheting heart.

'Absolutely.'

As she ordered she couldn't stop fretting that he wouldn't like her choices. She exhaled in relief when he proclaimed the Pinot Noir she had chosen perfect. But when his starter of rillettes and her warm artichoke salad arrived she pushed the food around her plate nervously.

'Aideen.'

She looked up at the command in his voice and her breath stalled when she looked into his formidable serious eyes.

'My food is delicious… Why are you so nervous?'

Giddy relief mixed with her trepidation, causing nervous energy to flow through her veins. She inhaled a shaky breath. 'I guess I'm waiting for an argument.'

'Is that what would have happened with your ex?'

'Yes.'

A tense silence settled between them. A quick glance told her that he was still studying her.

'How about we leave him in the past and you assume that I'm an okay guy?'

He said it with such quiet forcefulness that her stomach and heart did a simultaneous flip. God, he was right.

She lifted her head and met his gaze. 'You're right. And you're more than an okay guy.'

He gave a wry smile. 'I guess I don't have to worry about getting a big ego around you.'

With a cheeky grin she said, 'I compliment where it's deserved.'

'Are you telling me I have to work harder to earn your compliments?'

'Possibly.'

His eyebrow rose slowly and sexily and at the same time his eyes darkened. In a low, suggestive voice he said, 'I'll have to remember that.'

No! That wasn't what she'd meant! And why was she blushing? And why was her heart hammering in her chest? And did the couple next to them *have* to look so in love?

They spent the rest of the meal chatting about the countries they had visited, the movies they loved, the books they adored, but beneath all that civility a spiralling web of deep attraction was growing between them all the time. In every look, in every smile.

And the intimacy was only added to by her excitement at the amount of new books and places she had to try, based on his enthusiastic descriptions. It was as though a whole new and exciting world was opening up to her because of him.

'*Mademoiselle*, would you care to follow me to the kitchen?'

Confused, Aideen looked at their waiter. She'd only just noticed he was standing there, and said, 'Sorry…?'

'The chef is waiting for you.'

Perplexed, she looked towards Patrick, in the hope that he might understand what was going on.

With a sexy grin, his eyes alight with mischief, he said, 'Remember how you said you wanted to learn how to make a soufflé? Well, this restaurant is world-famous for them. You'll find no better place to learn.'

Dumbstruck, she stared at him. She leant towards him and whispered, 'What if I mess up? You've seen the way I work in the kitchen. This is a professional kitchen, for crying out loud. I might set off the fire alarm or something like that.'

'Maybe the chef will teach you how to work tidily as a bonus?'

She gave the waiter a quick smile and whispered impatiently, 'Patrick, I'm serious.'

He shook his head, amused. 'Go and have some fun. You're the one saying all the time that we both need to be spontaneous. Well, now's your chance.'

She sat back and took a deep breath. 'You're right.'

The waiter held her chair as she stood. She moved to the side of the table and leant over and kissed Patrick's cheek. 'This is the best surprise ever. Thank you.'

A while later Aideen returned to their table, triumphantly holding the biggest soufflé Patrick had ever seen, and smiling so brightly that the people at the tables around them burst into spontaneous applause. She took a playful bow, then sat and looked at the dessert, enraptured. The woman at the next table leant across and admired the creation, and Aideen enthusiastically described her experience in the kitchen.

He could not stop watching the delight dancing in her eyes, the warmth and humour with which she spoke to the other woman.

Two things hit him at once. First, the realisation that tonight wasn't just about helping Aideen and giving her support. He genuinely wanted to be in her company. He wanted to get to know her better. For the first time in years he had met someone he could talk to—a woman he deeply admired for her optimistic and determined take on life. And secondly the realisation came that he wanted her in his life as he'd never wanted a woman before.

Both things left him absolutely confounded.

CHAPTER EIGHT

ALL THE WAY home in the car they had chatted, and Patrick had teased her when she'd got Bernard to switch on the radio and then sang along to the old-time hits playing. He had declined her dare to join in, but Bernard had been a more willing singing partner, and by the end even Patrick had been humming along.

But now they were home that ease had vanished, and tension filled the air as they stood in the chateau's marble-floored entrance hall.

Silence wrapped around them and her stomach did a frenzy of flips when she looked up into the bright blue of his penetrating gaze. Dressed in a slim charcoal-grey suit and white shirt, he looked impossibly big and imposing.

Her insides went into freefall when his hand reached out and a finger trailed lightly against her forearm.

'I enjoyed tonight.'

Her body ached to fall against the hard muscle of his. To feel the crush of his mouth. But she didn't want to ruin what they had. Their blossoming…dared she say it?… *relationship* felt so fragile she was worried that taking it any further, complicating it, might pull it down like a house of cards.

So instead she gave him a big smile and said, 'It was fun. I don't think I've laughed so much in a long time.'

'Would you like a nightcap?'

She should just go to bed. They were on dangerous territory. She could see it in his blistering stare. This need for one another was a two-way street. Much as it pained her to do so, she needed to create a diversion—to call a halt to the chemistry fizzling between them.

'A nightcap sounds good. And I have a surprise I want to show you. I'll go and fetch it from my studio.'

'Now I'm intrigued. I'll fix us some drinks in the lounge.'

Walking towards the orangery, Aideen marvelled once again at the sheer scale of the chateau. What Patrick casually called 'the lounge' was a room at least five hundred feet square, with priceless parquet on the floor, littered with modern designer sofas and rugs, and with work from world-famous artists on the light grey walls.

As she reached for the surprise she had made for him on the trestle table, she hesitated and looked at it warily. Would he even like it? He could afford something encrusted in priceless jewels. Would he think this was laughable? Would he hate it? Her ex would have made some barbed comment that would have made her feel small and insignificant.

What was she thinking? She knew Patrick wasn't like that. He never intentionally hurt people. He was a kind man, with integrity. She had to stop letting her ex colour her judgement.

He watched her over the rim of his glass, desire flooding his veins, as she walked across the lounge floor to where he was sitting on a sofa; she looked incredibly beautiful.

Over cream wide-legged trousers she wore a vibrant lilac blouse, tucked into a thick band that displayed the narrow width of her waist.

Her hair was pulled back and twisted into a low coil at the back of her head, and he had spent the entire meal wondering what it would be like to press his lips to the pale column of her throat.

It was only as she drew nearer that he realised she was carrying something.

She stopped before him and gave him an uncertain smile before holding out a rectangular box. Then with a nervous frown she changed her mind and placed it on the beaten bronze coffee table in front of him before sitting opposite.

Covered in a pale blue and dark green silk fabric, in which the two colours ran into one another in layers, and the size of a shoe box, the box was too tempting not to open.

He sat forward and placed it on his lap. What could possibly be inside? He opened it up, fascinated. Inside it was lined in a rich dark navy velvet. And it was empty.

Confused he asked, 'What is it?'

'A memory chest for Orla's baby.'

He pulled the chest closer and made a pretence of inspecting it, his heart twisting at the reminder that he wouldn't be part of their lives.

In the periphery of his vision he could see Aideen's hands clasp her knees, her knuckles growing whiter and whiter.

'I was down in the village today and I saw the box in the little antique shop. It was originally lacquered on the outside, but I reckon too much handling and love over the years had damaged it beyond repair. When I saw it I thought it would be the perfect size for a memory chest for a baby. And it felt fitting to use a box that had been loved by someone before. The material I used to cover it was inspired by the sea and the land around Mooncoyne. I thought you might like to give it to Orla's baby…as a reminder of Mooncoyne, but also to keep up the tradition your dad started.'

He winced at her words, and she must have seen it, because at once she said with dismay, 'You don't like it.'

Seeing the chest had brought home just how much he hated the prospect of not being a part of his nephew's or niece's life. Anger towards Orla, and anger that they had lost their parents so young, had him saying crossly, 'It's not that. You shouldn't have bothered. It was a waste of your time. Orla will never accept it.'

'Why not?'

He put the chest back on the coffee table and reached for his brandy. 'It's too complicated to explain.'

She shuffled in her seat and he glanced at her. He looked away from the disappointment in her face.

She cleared her throat before she spoke. 'I know we're still getting to know one another…but I do want to help.'

He picked up the chest again and twisted it in his hands. Beneath the silk there was a thick layer of padding. No sharp corners that might hurt a baby.

'I'm guessing you spent hours making this?'

She tried to shrug it off. 'Not too long—just this afternoon. It was fun to do. But if you don't like it…'

His gaze shot up at the despondency in her voice. A wounded look clouded her eyes, but she gave him a resigned shrug. As though to say, *never mind*.

She had gone to a lot of effort. He wished she hadn't. But she deserved an explanation.

His throat felt peculiarly dry, and he wanted nothing but to get up and pace. But he forced himself to sit and talk to her, face to face.

'When my dad died Orla went from being outgoing and happy to an angry, rebellious teenager overnight. I was in my final year of university. I had already started a few companies on campus, and when I graduated—a few months after my dad died—I took them off campus and into my own headquarters. Orla moved to Dublin to live with me. We had no other family. From day one she fought me. She didn't like the school I selected for her. Some days I couldn't even get her to go. When she went out with friends she was constantly home late. Just to rile me, she started to date a series of unsuitable guys. Her school reports were appalling. When I tackled her about them she said she didn't care.'

Even remembering those days caused his pulse to quicken. He gritted his teeth and tried to inhale a calming breath.

'She had just lost her dad. School reports were probably way down on her agenda.'

His pulse spiked again. 'Do you think I didn't *know* that?'

She visibly jumped at his curt tone and he closed his eyes in exasperation.

'I'm sorry. That was uncalled for.'

She nodded her acceptance of his apology and waited for him to continue.

'I could see that she was hurting, but I knew her behaviour was going to hurt her even more in the long run. I had to stop her. I was, in effect, her parent. It was my duty to protect her, and I couldn't even get her out of bed in the morning.'

'But you told me before that you were only twenty-two.'

'That didn't matter.' He had been so full of dreams and ambitions that didn't involve a stroppy teenager. But he'd loved Orla, they'd had only one another, and he had given everything to trying to sort her out. Not that it had worked.

'Of course it mattered. How many twenty-two-year-olds are equipped to parent a teenager? It was a huge responsibility to take on.'

'What other choice did I have?'

She gave him a sympathetic look. 'I know. But don't downplay what you had to face. It was *huge*. Most people that age would have struggled. Many wouldn't have taken it on.' She paused for a minute, and then said in a quiet voice, 'It must have been a really difficult time for you both.'

'Yes, it was. I was getting pressure from her school. Work was crazy. I had to travel, so I employed a house-keeper—in truth she was a trained nanny, but I couldn't tell Orla that. She, too, constantly struggled with Orla. I used to come home from travelling, exhausted, to a sister who used to yell at me that she hated me. That I wasn't her dad and I should stop trying to act like it.'

'What did you argue about?'

'Everything. Her clothes, her going out, her curfew, the housekeeper… But the biggest thing was her refusal to go to school.'

'Did you consider moving her to a different school? Maybe she wasn't happy there?'

'After the fight I'd had to get her into that school there was no way I was moving her. It was the best school in Dublin. And she wouldn't even give it a chance. I told her she had to give it a year, but she wouldn't listen.'

'What do you mean, it was the best school in Dublin?'

'It was consistently in the top three for academic results in the entire country.'

'Was Orla academic? Are you certain the school suited her?'

He looked skywards. 'She would have been academic if she had applied herself. Instead she spent her days stockpiling make-up and texting on her phone. In the end I even moved us to a different part of the city, where she didn't have as many distractions. I confiscated her phone and stopped her allowance, but she still fought me all the way.'

'Maybe you should have given her some say in what school she went to. Included her in the decision-making. She had lost her dad, moved away from her friends...my guess is she was feeling pretty confused. Did you both talk through all that?'

'I was up to my eyes with work. And any time we spoke she ended up storming off, refusing to speak to me.'

'When I was that age most sixteen-year-olds I knew were pretty good at looking after themselves and knowing what they needed.'

She paused and rubbed her hands up and down the soft cream wool material of her trousers before giving him a tentative smile.

'I know this is easy for me to say, standing on the outside... Heaven knows, I'm only too aware how easy it is to get caught up in the messy dynamics of a relationship... how acute the hurt can be when it's someone we really care about... It can be hard to think objectively, to understand where we went wrong, how we could do things differently in the future.'

Again she paused, and gave him an apologetic smile, as though to forewarn him that he wasn't going to like what she was about to say.

She inhaled a deep breath. 'But maybe you should have allowed her to make some of the decisions herself... or made a joint decision. Not you deciding everything, controlling everything.'

His spine arched defensively at her words. 'I had to protect her.'

'Maybe she needed her big brother more than she needed a father figure... She was grieving for her dad. She would probably have resisted anyone who tried taking his place. I know I would.'

Some of what she'd said was starting to make him feel really uncomfortable. He hated remembering that time—how he'd floundered, the frustration of knowing he was losing Orla day by day.

As much to her as himself, he said, 'So it was all my fault?'

She moved to the edge of the sofa. 'No. Not at all. You were worried about her, and understandably wanted to do right by her. Protect her. But maybe you should have stopped and tried to understand what she needed, rather than what you *thought* she needed.'

'Well, she has made it pretty clear that now she needs me out of her life. Two years ago she left for Madrid, and now she rarely answers my calls. Before our dad died we were so close—she used to tell me everything. Now we have nothing.'

'Maybe the baby will bring you both closer?'

He gave a sharp laugh. 'I don't think so. She was over five months pregnant before I found out. And that was only because I flew over to see her. She admitted she hadn't planned on telling me. And she wouldn't tell me who the father is.'

'Why is that of any importance?'

She *had* to be kidding. 'Because he left her—the coward. And I would like to have a word with him and set him straight on parental responsibility.'

At that she smiled, and then her smile broke into laughter. He watched her, bewildered. And then he got it. He sounded like an old-fashioned controlling father.

He rolled his eyes. 'Next thing I'll be marching them both up the aisle, a shotgun in my arms.'

This only made her laugh even more. It lifted the whole mood in the room and gave him a little perspective.

'Okay, tracking down the father isn't going to be on my list of priorities.'

'Glad to hear it.' Her head tilted and she gave him a small smile. 'I really admire how you took on the responsibility of caring for Orla. You did your best in very difficult circumstances. My take on it, for what it's worth, is that if you stop pushing she'll come back to you. We all need and want family support. It's not something we naturally walk away from. And now that Orla is having a baby she needs your support more than ever before.'

He had to admire her optimism. 'I think things are too fractured for that.'

'You were the one who said you admired me for restarting my business. How about you try to restart your relationship with Orla? Think about what you would do differently so that you can have a better relationship with her.'

She made it sound so simple. 'I don't know...I don't want to upset her at this late stage of her pregnancy.'

'I understand that, but she needs you.'

'Orla wouldn't agree with you, I'm afraid.'

Even he heard the exhaustion in his own voice. He stared up at the ceiling. His little sister…pregnant. He just couldn't get his head around it. How would their dad have reacted? He would have worried, but supported Orla one hundred per cent. His dad had had unconditional love down to an art form.

Across from him, Aideen sighed. 'Patrick, I really think you need to cut yourself some slack. You were only in your early twenties. You were running several rapidly expanding multimillion-pound businesses and trying to parent a teenage girl. You did your best. Sure, you made mistakes. Haven't we all? But, as you've said to me, that's in the past. Focus on the future now. You have to think about the next generation in your family. Your nephew or niece will need you. Orla's baby deserves to have you in its life.'

His gut tightened. She was right. But what if he caused Orla more upset? What if they had yet another bitter argument? He would never forgive himself if something happened to her or the baby because of him.

He picked up the chest, the material smooth against his skin. 'I would like to keep this, if that's okay with you. Hopefully some day I'll get the chance to give it to Orla and her baby. It's beautifully made.'

He genuinely looked as though he loved the chest, and Aideen prayed that a time would come when he could give it to Orla. She could see how much the rift was hurting him.

'Were the arguments with Orla one of the reasons why you moved to Ashbrooke?'

'Partially… And in truth they prompted my move here to the chateau, as well. I love both houses, and I'm proud of the restoration I've carried out at Ashbrooke. It would have been terrible to see it fall into further decay when it's of such historic importance. At the same time, I *did* need to retreat and focus on my businesses. They were growing at a rate even I hadn't anticipated. But I also needed some head space after years of arguing with Orla. My apartments both in Dublin and in Paris held too many memories. Orla moved to Paris and lived in my apartment when she was expelled from school. It was pretty tense, to say the least—especially when I arrived to find she had moved two friends in with her.'

'You didn't tell me that she was expelled.'

'Amongst other things. She came to Paris to attend a language school, but she dropped out of there, too. She said she'd learn French faster working in a bar.'

She didn't understand why he sounded so exasperated. 'But that was *good*—she was taking on responsibility for herself and learning to be independent.'

'You didn't see the bar she was working in.'

'Am I right in guessing you didn't allow her to keep working there?'

'Too right. She was on the first plane back to Ireland.'

'How old was she?'

'Eighteen.'

She inhaled a deep breath. 'Were there any other options other than sending her home? She was an adult, after all.'

'She certainly wasn't *acting* like an adult.'

'Did sending her back to Ireland work? Did it help your relationship?'

He glanced at her briefly and then looked away. 'No.'

'Would you do anything differently if you had that time again?'

He looked thrown by her question. For a good few minutes they sat in silence, his gaze trained on a spot in the far distance.

'I would do a lot of things differently.'

His thumb travelled again over the silk of the chest, and when he looked up she realised the pale blue of the material was a close match to the colour of his eyes.

He held her gaze and said, 'You're the first person I've ever told any of this to.'

'What do you mean?'

'Exactly that. I never told anyone about the problems we were having.'

'Not the school or your friends?'

'No.'

'You mean you carried all of this on your own?'

'Orla and I only had one another. It didn't seem right to tell anyone else what was happening. It was private—between the two of us. Family problems should stay within the walls of a home.'

'But not something as big as this, Patrick. Not when you're on your own, with no one to ask for advice or just talk it through with. It must have been so tough for you.'

Bittersweet sadness caught in her chest. She was honoured and moved that he had told her. But she also felt a heavy sadness that he had been burdened with this for so long.

'You shouldn't have carried it on your own.'

A solemn, serious gaze met hers. 'I could level the same accusation at you.'

Emotion took a firm grip of her throat. 'You're right… It's hard to speak when you're hurting, when you're embarrassed and loaded down with guilt.'

'I'm glad I did tell you.' A smile played at the corner

of his mouth and he added, 'I never thought I would say this, but it's actually a relief to talk about it.'

It felt so good to see him smile. 'I'm glad, too.'

He considered her for a while, and her cheeks began to flame at the way his eyes darkened. An emotional connection pinged between them and her heart slowed to a solid throb.

In a low voice he said, 'I've been thinking over what you said about having more fun, and I've lined up a surprise for you tomorrow.'

Her heart began to race again, and to cover the wide smile of excitement that threatened to break on her mouth at any second she eyed him suspiciously. 'I hope it's not a triathlon, or something crazy like that.'

He shook his head with amusement, 'No, but I reckon you'd be pretty lethal in a triathlon—if the competitive way you play tennis is anything to go by.'

'You might be right, but I'm not the best of swimmers.'

'Really? You can't live by the sea and not be able to swim! When we get back to Ashbrooke I'll give you some lessons in the lough.'

Was he serious? He seemed to be. Mixed emotions assailed her at once, and a crazy excitement to know that he would want to do something like that. That there might be some type of future for them beyond Paris.

But what if she was wrong? Was she reading way too much into this? Was she crazy to believe and trust in a man enough to even *contemplate* the possibility of some type of future with him?

Her doubts and fears won out and she dismissed his suggestion with a laugh, praying it would mask the embarrassing frozen expression of hope on her face. 'Only if I can wear a wetsuit. The water is pretty cold in the lough.'

'Wimp!'

'I am not. Anyway, I have meetings tomorrow until four. Can the surprise wait until then?'

'Perfect. I'll collect you.'

She stood up and said happily, 'It's a date. Now I'm going to bed.'

Only as she went to walk away did she realise what she had said.

'Not that it's really a date or anything like that… You know what I mean.'

He, too, stood, and looked at her fondly, laughter in his eyes. 'Aideen…relax. And I would *like* it to be a date.'

'Would you?'

He pinned her with his gaze. 'Yes.'

His answer was such a low, sexy drawl that goose-bumps popped up on her skin. She gave him a skittish grin and before she embarrassed herself any further decided to make a hasty retreat. But not before she threw him another goofy smile.

As she walked out of the room she heard him say in the same sexy tone, 'Goodnight, Aideen. Sleep well.'

A delicious, deep shiver of anticipation ran the length of her body.

CHAPTER NINE

THE FOLLOWING EVENING at Issy-les-Moulineaux heliport, close to the Eiffel Tower, a helicopter stood awaiting their arrival.

As Bernard brought the car to a halt beside the impressive machine excitement bubbled in Aideen's veins. 'Where are we going?'

Patrick considered her mischievously as he contemplated her question. 'Now, if I told you that it wouldn't be much of a surprise, would it?'

'The helicopter is enough of a surprise for me... Oh, please tell me! I hate being kept in suspense.'

'No can do, I'm afraid. The good things in life come to those who wait.'

Bernard was waiting patiently at the door for her to exit, so she stepped out of the car. When Patrick joined her and they walked towards the helicopter she asked playfully, 'So is that your philosophy on life?'

He brought them both to a stop and stepped closer. He leant down. His breath was warm against her ear when he spoke and her heart did a triple flip.

'Sometimes the anticipation and the wait can be thrilling, don't you agree?'

Heat erupted in her body and she drew back to meet

his eyes, which blistered into hers. When she finally managed to speak it was in an embarrassingly squeaky voice. 'I guess...'

His gaze changed to a look of amusement and, taking her hand in his, he led her to the helicopter, where the pilot was waiting for them with the rear door open.

As the pilot made the final checks for take-off her mind raced. Was he confirming what she suspected... that he would like more with her? She had read signals so wrongly in the past. Was she getting this wrong, too? But the way he looked at her said she wasn't getting anything wrong. He looked at her as though he would like to bed her then and there.

For the entire forty-five-minute journey they played a game of 'yes and no' in which she tried to guess their destination. She was wrong on every count, and was rapidly running out of names. It was a good job she had listened in her geography lessons in school.

But when a baroque castle appeared in the distance, with its raked roof and tall chimney stacks, she whispered, 'Oh, my...it's Château de Chalant.'

Privately owned by the Forbin family, Château de Chalant was considered one of the most beautiful castles in France. It was never open to the public.

'What are we doing here?'

'Frédéric Forbin is a friend and business associate. I called him and arranged for us to visit the chateau.'

Flabbergasted, she could only stare at him, and then down at the manicured elegant grounds as the helicopter swept towards the chateau. As the helicopter landed, she saw a man waiting for them at the bottom of the steps leading up to a terrace that then led to double wooden front door.

'Is that Frédéric?'

'No, it's the chateau director, who is expecting us. Frédéric is away travelling. The chateau is of such historical and architectural importance Frédéric employs a conservation team, headed by the director.'

As they exited the helicopter she tried to dampen down the enthusiasm fizzing in her blood. She had studied the historic textiles of Château de Chalant while at university. Now she was going to see them first-hand! She wanted to babble with excitement, but forced herself to shake the director's hand calmly.

Then both men shook hands.

'Monsieur Fitzsimon, it is a pleasure to have you back at Château de Chalant. It's been a long time.'

'Good to see you, too, Edouard.'

There was a slight catch to his voice, but despite that Patrick looked totally at ease and in no way fazed, as she was by the grandeur of the chateau. Once again she was struck by how different his life was from hers—how used he was to mixing in the world of wealth and power.

Edouard led them into the vast entrance hall of the chateau, where two sweeping marble stone staircases, one at either side, led up to a wooden gallery that encircled the hall. Historic tapestries hung from the walls.

Unable to help herself, she walked to a sixteenth-century oak chair and exclaimed, 'Oh, wow! That chair is upholstered in Avalan fabric. I've never seen it in real life before; only in textbooks.'

The director looked at her in surprise. 'Not many people would recognise this fabric—are you a historian?'

'No, I'm a textile designer, but I have a passion for historical fabrics. I love how designs and patterns tell us so much about the period of history they were produced in, about the social norms and conditions.'

'Well, you're in for a treat this evening.' The director turned to Patrick. 'I will leave you and Mademoiselle Ryan to tour the chateau alone. If you need anything I shall be in my office.'

As they walked away from the entrance hall she asked, intrigued, 'Why did you bring me here?'

'This is the most beautiful building I have ever visited. I thought you would enjoy it. But now I'm especially glad that I organised the trip. I hadn't realised you were so passionate and knowledgeable about historical textiles.'

'I have a lot of hidden talents you don't know about.'

With a glint in his eye he said, 'Is that right?'

She mumbled, 'Yes...' and turned away, heat flooding her cheeks. She felt as though she was floating on air between the excitement of being here and her desperation to feel his lips on hers again, to be encompassed by his size and strength.

He was right. Anticipation was thrilling. But what if that anticipation led to nothing?

The first room he took her to was the print room. As Aideen looked around the room in astonishment he explained, 'It was a tradition for royalty and the gentry to collect expensive prints and paste them directly on to the walls.'

Some of the black and white prints illustrated far-away picturesque locations—the lakes of Northern Italy, Bavarian forests... Animal prints showed farmyard scenes of cows and sheep; another was of a spaniel, standing before a raging river.

She was blown away by the sheer extravagance of the room. Priceless print after print covered the entirety of the four walls. 'They're beautiful—what incredible detail.'

'This room was created by Princess Isabella—it's said Prince Henri of Chalant built this chateau as a symbol of his love for her, before they married.'

'That's so romantic.'

He didn't respond, and when she turned to him the air was compressed in her lungs. He stood in the middle of the room, his hands in his pockets, gazing at her intently. He wore navy chinos and a white polo shirt. His bare arms were beautifully carved with taut muscle, the skin lightly tanned with a dusting of dark hair.

She even fancied his arms. Was there any hope for her?

An awareness passed between them and she suddenly grew shy, giving him a quick smile before walking away to inspect other prints.

But he made for the door and gestured her to follow. 'If you think that's romantic let me show you something else.'

She followed him down the corridor until he stopped at a closed door.

'Close your eyes and I'll lead you in.'

She eyed him suspiciously. 'You're not going to play a trick on me, are you? Lead me down into the dungeon or something like that?'

His head tilted and he gave her a sexy grin that sent her pulse into orbit. 'As intriguing as that suggestion sounds… no, I'm not going to take you to the dungeon.' Then he gave her an admonishing look and said, 'Now, for once will you please try and trust me and close your eyes?'

She held her breath as his hand took hers. She heard the door open and then he slowly led her forward for about ten paces. She felt oddly vulnerable, and her hand tightened on his of its own accord.

All her senses were attuned to the solid strength of his hand, the smooth warmth of his skin, the torturous pleasure of being so physically close to him...

'Open your eyes.'

She gasped in astonishment. It was the most dazzling room she'd ever seen. It was like something out of a fairytale. Or a room she imagined might have been in a Russian royal palace.

She twisted around in amazement, shaking her head. The double-height rectangular room was a feast of gilded Baroque plasterwork. It was opulent and outrageous in its beauty. And so much fun she couldn't help but laugh.

'It's absolutely stunning! It's like standing in the middle of an exquisite piece of twenty-four-carat gold jewellery'

'It's called the Gold Room. Prince Henri commissioned it to celebrate Isabella's fiftieth birthday.'

She gave him a wistful smile. 'He really was romantic, wasn't he?'

He gave a light shrug and looked up at the intricate gilt stucco work on the ceiling. 'I guess when you find the love of your life you just want to celebrate it.'

A rush of emotion tore through her body. 'It must be nice to feel so loved.'

Their eyes met briefly and they both looked away at the same time.

She moved through the silent room, unexpected tears clouding her vision. The past year might have made her wary of others, but at the same time there was an emptiness in her heart. She wanted to be in love. Desperately.

With each passing day, as they got to know each other,

things were changing between her and Patrick. They now shared an intimacy, an ease with one another that had her thinking maybe they had something between them... something significant. Patrick telling her last night about Orla had been particularly moving, and also momentous. It was as though he had finally allowed her to step fully into his life.

Behind her, he called, 'Are you ready to see some more rooms?'

She nodded, but was slow to turn around. Was he feeling the same intensity she was? This need to connect on a different level?

An hour later her head swam as she tried once again to orientate herself in the vastness of the chateau. They had passed through room after room, all full of sumptuous furniture and historically significant textiles and antiques. And yet, somewhat miraculously, Château Chalant retained an air of intimacy. Was it because it had been built to celebrate love?

Eventually they found themselves back in the entrance hall. For some reason she didn't want their time here to end. She wanted to stay here with him a little longer.

With a heavy heart she said, as brightly as she could, 'Thank you for bringing me here—it really is a magical place.'

'The tour isn't over yet. I have kept the best room for last.'

Intrigued, she followed him into a vast, empty room with marble flooring. A bow window overlooked the gardens to the rear of the chateau.

She looked around, perplexed, taking in the ornate plasterwork on the domed ceilings and alcoves. Painted a silvery white, the sunlit room was a sleeping silent oasis, even in the tranquillity of the chateau.

'Why is there no furniture?' She jumped to hear her own voice echoing noisily around the room.

He had remained standing close to the doorway, while she was now perched on the sill of the bow window.

'It helps with the acoustics.'

What had been a whisper from Patrick echoed loudly across the room.

Trying it herself, she whispered, 'This is amazing.'

Again her voice barrelled across the room in a loud echo.

'It's called the Whispering Room. In days gone by apparently it wasn't accepted for courting couples to stand too close to one another, so young lovers would use this room to whisper messages to one another.'

'That's so sweet.'

'I sometimes wonder what they would have said.'

As he stood and watched her something broke inside her, and she whispered from her heart. 'They wished they could be together...they longed for the day they could be.'

For the longest while he stared at her. Had he heard her whisper? Maybe it would be better if he hadn't.

But then he whispered back, 'You're lovely.'

He said it so gently and with such sincerity she thought her heart was going to break in two. 'You're pretty special, too.'

'I like you, Aideen Ryan.'

Had she heard right? Had she imagined it? His smile said otherwise.

Through a throat thick with bittersweet happiness she whispered, 'I like you, too, Patrick Fitzsimon.'

He walked slowly to her, and although she was leaning against the windowsill her legs began to wobble.

He came to a stop before her and she looked up into his dazzling blue eyes. His body shifted towards her. His hand twitched at his side and at the same time her body ached with the need for his touch.

His head moved slowly down, her heart speeding up with every inch closer he came, until his lips landed gently on hers. His mouth moved against hers, slowly and lightly, and she thought she might faint because it was so tender and right.

When he pulled away from the kiss he brought his forehead to lie against hers. His incredible blue gaze held hers. It felt as though he was spearing her heart with the silent communication of the need of a man for a woman.

'Would you like a tour of the grounds?'

Dazed, she whispered, 'Yes, please.'

They made their way through the extensive gardens surrounding the chateau and a silence fell between them. She tried to keep her distance from him, but invariably found herself swaying towards him. As she walked along the gravelled paths, the late-evening sun warm on her skin, she bumped against him and he pulled her towards him, wrapping his arm about her waist. They shared a quick look and her insides tumbled to see the desire in his hooded eyes.

She felt drunk with happiness just being there...being with him. And every cell in her body was electrified by being so close to him. A lazy, intoxicating tendril of physical desire coiled around her body. Her skin felt flushed and a deep pulse resonated in her lips.

But that nagging thought that this was not reality, that

she did not belong here, continued to rumble at the back of her brain. Even as she tried her best to ignore it.

They didn't stop walking until they reached an extensive lake with a small island in the centre. They stopped on the pebbled beach, where a rowing boat lay beached to one side.

He went immediately to it and pulled it towards the lake. Holding it in the water, he called, 'Come on—what are you waiting for?'

She looked around doubtfully, wondering for a moment if it would be allowed. But then she rushed towards the water. She pulled off her ballet flats, held up her midiskirt and jumped on board, giving a cry of laughter when the boat wobbled.

Patrick strengthened his grip on her elbow, and as she sat down he pushed the boat out further and in one fluid motion jumped on board himself. The boat wobbled even more, but as soon as he sat opposite her it steadied.

His oar strokes were long and even and they were quickly out in the middle of the lake. Other than evening birdsong and the swoosh of the oars in the water there wasn't another sound.

'This is my first time ever being out in a rowing boat.'

He looked at her incredulously. 'Seriously? How did you get to be…?'

'Twenty-eight.'

'How did you get to be twenty-eight without ever being out in a rowing boat?'

'Beats me.'

He continued to row and she tried not to stare at the way his biceps flexed with each pull of the oar.

'You'll have to have a go at rowing.'

'Really?'

'Climb over here into the centre. Try not to wobble the boat too much. I'll move to your seat.'

As she moved down the boat it began to bob precariously. She gave a little shout of alarm and gratefully grabbed on to his outstretched arm. As she fell forward she twisted, and ended up landing in his arms, her bottom firmly wedged in his lap.

His hand came to rest just above her waist, its heat on the thin cotton of her blouse sending a shiver of pleasure through her. His thighs, his chest, as they pressed against her, felt as though they were made of steel. Electric blue eyes met hers. Her pulse leapt. It would be so easy to lean forward, to kiss those firm lips again. To inhale his scent.

He gave a low growl. 'If you don't climb off me in the next five seconds I won't be responsible for what I do next.'

She leapt away—and instantly regretted doing so.

After he had moved to the stern of the boat she started rowing. The boat moved with ease and she thought with unjustified satisfaction that she had this rowing lark immediately sussed. But then they started going in circles, and she couldn't get the boat to go in a straight line. The fits of giggles that accompanied her attempts weren't much help.

Opposite her, he threw his head into his hands and then looked at her with amusement.

Time and time again he demonstrated the motion she should be using, but the boat still twisted. He suggested they swop places again but, determined, she refused to give up.

And finally she did it. The boat went in one direction. Straight back to shore. She didn't try to alter their course in case she started circling again.

As they neared the small beach he moved confidently to the bow and jumped ashore. Then he hoisted the boat on to the stones. He held her hand as she leapt off. She knew she was grinning at him like a fool but couldn't stop herself. She hadn't laughed so much in a very long time.

He watched her with a smile, and for a while she looked at him happily, but her smile finally faded as his stare grew darker. He took a step closer. Shots of awareness flew through her.

An intensity swirled in the air between them. Everything had changed since Patrick had opened up to her last night. She felt trusted. Her heart drummed a slow beat of deep appreciation, wonder, and attraction to this man.

Closer and closer he came, his intense blue eyes transfixing her. Her breath grew more rapid. Her lips pulsed with the need to feel his mouth on hers again. Her legs grew weak.

When he was no more than an inch from her, she was the first to give in. Her body swayed and she fell against his hardness. Her hands curled around his biceps. Against her thumb, which rested at the side of his chest, she could feel his heartbeat, which was pounding even faster than hers.

'I didn't ask before, so I should this time round. Can I kiss you?'

Her heart stuttered at his question. It was the sweetest thing anyone had ever said to her. Even if she'd wanted to there was no way she could pull away from him—from his warm breath, the overwhelming pull of his hard body, the dizzying inhalation of his scent.

She placed her hands on his shoulders, closed her eyes, and gave a small sigh of assent as she pulled his lips down to hers.

Whereas their earlier kiss had been slow and sweet, tentative and testing, this kiss was instantly intense, wild. Their hands explored each other's bodies with hunger. It was a kiss that might easily become a lot more.

She was quickly losing herself.

As one, they pulled away at the same time. As though they both knew it might quickly spiral into something neither wanted...*yet*.

She pressed a hand to her swollen lips and blushed. She had to hide how much he affected her. Because in truth she was close to tears...of happiness and despair.

'I'll tell you this much, Patrick Fitzsimon, you certainly haven't forgotten how to kiss in all that time you've been locked away in your office.'

He looked at her with amusement. 'Glad to hear it.'

But then dark need flared in his eyes and her insides melted.

'I want you, Aideen.'

Her heart felt as if it was going to burst right out of her chest. She so desperately wanted to say *Yes, please* and not give a thought to the consequences. But it wasn't that simple.

'Are you sure? Won't it...complicate things?'

His hand came to rest on her cheek and he gazed at her solemnly while his thumb stroked her skin. 'I like you. A lot. It doesn't have to be complicated. I promise you, no game playing. But if this is not right for you I'll back off.'

No! She didn't want that.

His touch, his scent, the magnetic pull of his body might be making her head reel so much that she could barely formulate a thought, but she knew that much. She didn't want this to end.

When he had whispered 'I like you' in the Whispering Room, he had looked at her with such intense integrity and honour it had been like a bomb detonating in her brain. And just like that she'd realised she was in love with this kind, generous, strong man. And, God help her, she knew she would happily take a few days in his arms over the alternative: never knowing what it would be like to be held by him.

Right now, to have loved and lost was definitely better than never to have loved at all. She didn't want to think about the future. Living in the present was all that mattered.

She scrunched her eyes shut for a moment, and when she opened them again she said, with a huge smile, 'Okay.'

It was as though a weight had been lifted off her shoulders. She had never felt so exhilarated in her entire life. To feel this good it must mean it was the right decision. Mustn't it?

All the way back to Paris she regaled him with stories of her encounters with fashion designers. He held her hand throughout, his thumb caressing the soft smoothness of her palm, and every now and again she would stutter and lose her train of thought as his fingers lightly traced along her inner arm.

Each time she shivered and her eyes grew heavy he wondered if her entire body was that sensitive. And his pulse moved up another notch.

When the helicopter landed Bernard was waiting to take them to his private club, close to the Eiffel Tower.

She gasped beside him when the maître d' of the club's restaurant directed them to their table in the rooftop terrace restaurant. And he totally understood why. Because, no matter how many times he came here himself, the sheer size and beauty of the Eiffel Tower this close up was truly impressive.

Their table, as he'd requested, was beside the low-level redbrick wall of the terrace, with her chair facing out towards the tower, he sitting to her side.

Once the maître d' had gone she stared at him, her huge chocolate eyes dancing in merriment, and then she put a hand over her mouth in disbelief. 'Oh, my God, I can't believe this place. It's incredible.'

'The club is one of the closest buildings to the tower.'

Their waiter arrived with the champagne he had pre-ordered and opened the bottle with a satisfying pop. He filled the flute glasses that already sat on the white-linen-topped table and retreated once he had placed the bottle in an ice bucket to the side.

She took a sip of champagne. And then another. 'Wow! That's the nicest champagne I have ever tasted. It's sharp, but with a gorgeous biscuit undertone.' She turned again to the tower and reached her hand out towards it. 'I feel like I can almost touch it.'

Then, as she looked around the rest of the terrace, he saw her expression grow even more radiant.

'This club is so impressive—' She stopped and blushed, and dropped her chin on to her cupped hand. 'Oh, dear. I must sound like the most uncultured date you've ever had.'

'You make a refreshing change from some of the jaded dates I've had in the past.'

She gave him a suspicious look. 'That's good…I think.'

If only she knew how many times in the past he had been left speechless by the cynicism and sense of entitlement of some of his previous conquests. 'That's *very* good.'

As they both leant forward to place their glasses on the table their arms touched and a silent energy bound them together. He moved closer and her lips parted ever so slightly. Hunger powered through him. He inhaled her scent. The scent that now lingered in the air of the chateau and one he looked forward to inhaling each day when he returned from his meetings.

Slowly their heads moved towards one another. Her head tilted to the side and passion flared in her eyes. Inch by inch they drew closer, and he had to stifle a groan when his lips met the soft fullness of hers.

When he pulled away he was amused by how dazed she looked, and said, 'You're the best date I've ever had.'

She blushed furiously and waved away his words, but her wide smile told of her delight.

A group of waiters arrived with the food he had also pre-ordered, earlier in the day. The surprise and glee with which she eyed the food had him smiling to himself in pleasure.

Once the waiters had departed she looked mischievously from the tiers of mouth-watering cakes to him. 'It's a bit late in the evening for afternoon tea, I would have thought.'

'You said you loved millefeuille.'

Shaking her head, she bent to inspect the three-tier stand. 'All the cakes I used to dream of when I was a student: opera cake, éclairs, *macarons*…even miniature tarte Tatin.' She looked at him, her throat working. 'Thank you.' She stopped as tears filled her eyes. 'This is so considerate of you…' And then she laughed. 'I'm actually lost for words.'

He gave her a smile. 'Then don't speak. Just eat.'

He poured her some tea while she selected a mille-feuille. He chose a raspberry *macaron*, filled with fresh raspberries and raspberry cream.

She closed her eyes as she ate the first forkful of millefeuille. And he almost choked on his *macaron*. She looked incredibly sensual, with her head tilted back, pleasure written all over her face. He glared at a man sitting at a nearby table who was also captivated by her, a powerful surge of possessiveness taking him by surprise.

Her happiness was increasingly becoming everything to him. It was as though he was plugged into her emotions and felt them as keenly as she did. When she was happy he was elated. When she was sad or upset his heart plummeted. He had never before felt so attuned to another person.

It was both incredible and awful at the same time. Incredible that he could be so close to another person that he felt her emotions. Awful because it would make saying goodbye all the more difficult.

As they ate they spoke about their past experiences in Paris, with the tower lighting up before them as the sun set. They both looked towards its graceful night-time beauty, but he quickly looked back at her.

Her eyes shone with happiness. She was curled into her seat so that her body was directed towards him, even though her gaze was still on the tower. Her lipstick had faded from brilliant red to a faint blush.

Unable to stop himself, he leant towards her and said her name gently. She turned to face him fully with a smile and his hand reached forward to brush a flake of pastry from her lips. At least that was what he intended to do.

He removed the pastry, all right, but his finger lingered on her lips, desire coiling in his stomach.

At first she stared at him in surprise, but then her gaze darkened. He lowered his finger but moved forward in his chair, wanting to be closer to her...

Awareness of his masculinity, of his raw power, flooded Aideen's body and her head began to swim at the heat and scent of his skin.

'I want you.'

It was the barest of whispers and she drew back a little, needing to search his eyes, to see if she had heard right. The hooded intensity there told her she had heard correctly.

Her throat was too dry to speak so she mouthed the words *me, too.*

His eyes darkened even more as they traced the movement of her lips.

Immediately he stood and held out his hand to her. Her insides had gone all funny and she worried that her legs wouldn't carry her.

Just as they were about to leave, the tower started its hourly light show, and as she stood watching the twinkling lights, enraptured, he held her from behind, his hands encircling her waist, his thumbs drawing lazy sensual patterns up and over her ribs.

In the back of the car she tried not to tremble as he held her hand. Silent, powerful restraint pulsated from his rigid body.

Once home, he threw open the front door and pulled her into the darkness, backed her against the wall.

He stood so close the heat from his body curled around her, and she gasped when his fingers moved to undo the top buttons of her blouse. Once open, he pulled it down to expose both shoulders. Slowly he left a trail of soft, knee-weakening kisses along her collarbone and the sensitive ridge of her neck, his fingers dragging down the apricot-coloured lace straps of her bra, leaving a burning trail of heat on her skin.

A deep moan of pleasure ricocheted from deep inside her. Her fingers scratched against the cool wall at her back, desperate to cling to anything.

'I want to make love to you.'

For the longest while she fought to answer him, her mind distracted as he continued to caress her earlobe, her neck.

The absolute gorgeousness of inhaling him... The bone-melting thrill of his large, muscular body being so close... The desperate need to touch every inch of him... To have his body crushed against hers. To have him make love to her.

Her hands clasped his face and drew him up to face her. Her breath hitched as his burning gaze met hers.

'I want you, too.'

CHAPTER TEN

A BUBBLE OF happiness and excitement burst in Aideen's heart and spread little beads of serenity throughout her body.

Beside her, twisted on to his side and facing away from her, Patrick slept, his breathing a slow and steady rhythm. The top sheet rested below his waist, and the beautiful, muscular expanse of his back was only inches away.

In the pre-dawn light she could just about make out the faint scar that ran for a few inches just below his shoulderblade. What had caused it? There was so much she wanted to know about him. So much more to fall in love with. Simple everyday events like him brushing his teeth, the order in which he dressed, shaved.

She moved closer and lowered her head against the hard muscles of his back, inhaling the musky, salty notes of his scent which always made her light-headed with desire.

Last night had been more exhilarating and tender than she'd ever thought possible. They had made love slowly and gently, with an intensity that had had her fearing her heart would split in two. With each kiss and touch she had tried to show him what he meant to her, hoping he would see just how much she loved his strength and dignity, loved his kindness and integrity.

Throughout he had whispered words of endearment to her, his eyes dark with passion...and also with the same amazement and wonder that had had her reeling, too.

And as she fell back to sleep, as she fell into a contented, exhausted pit of happiness, she wished she could stay there, in his bed, at his side, for eternity.

Two hours later the morning sun bathed the bedroom in a golden light. In their haste they had not got around to pulling the curtains last night.

Lying on her stomach, Aideen was sleeping, her skin still flushed from their lovemaking. He leant forward and touched his mouth against hers. Her lips broke into a smile and her eyes opened, drowsy and lazy with happiness.

She gave him a contented sexy sigh. 'Good morning.'

The huskiness of her voice evoked startling images of their lovemaking last night. Images that left him reeling in disbelief and with the desire to experience it time and time again. He lowered his head and kissed the warm skin of her shoulderblade. A ribbon of pleasure unfurled in him when he inhaled the fresh vanilla and floral scent that seemed innate to her very being.

Against the sweet scent of her skin he whispered, 'Good morning to you, too.'

She edged her hip closer to him as his hand ran over her back. Her eyes met his and they shared a look so intimate it felt as though the world had stopped turning.

Eventually he found his voice. 'Did you enjoy last night?'

She looked at him innocently. 'Best night's sleep I've had in a long time.'

For that, he kissed her hard, and he didn't stop until he heard her whimper with need. When he pulled away she protested, and then nudged even closer to him, the length of her body tucking into his.

A sexy wickedness flashed on her face. 'Okay, I'll admit that it was pretty mind-blowing.'

A deep groan erupted from the core of him. He pressed his mouth against the side of her throat. He ran his hand down over her back, his thumb bumping along her spine so that she wriggled, and she wriggled even more when the entire span of his hand moved down over the firm roundness of her bottom.

'Have I ever told you that you have an incredible body?'

Her giggle echoed off the mattress and her body shimmied beneath his fingers.

'As I recall, you said something to that effect several times last night.'

'Well, you'd better get used to it, because I reckon I'm going to keep you in this bed for a very long time.'

She gave a heavy sigh and smiled. 'That sounds like heaven. Being with you is incredible. I never want it to end.'

His hand stilled and his heart sank. He'd thought this was nothing but banter and teasing. But now her words echoed in his brain. They both knew this was never going to last. Didn't they?

He glanced at her again and the joy in her eyes had turned to disquiet. Her brow drew into a frown. She twisted on to her back, pulling the sheet up around her as she did so.

'What's the matter?'

He collapsed on to his back, too, and stared up to the ceiling. 'You know this has to end… I thought we were agreed on that?'

He felt her yank the sheet a little tighter about her. 'I know. But after last night…'

After last night? Panic and disbelief had him sitting up on the side of the bed.

Without turning to face her, he said, 'I have a conference call in ten minutes. I need to get ready.'

She didn't respond, and he walked rapidly to the en-suite bathroom. He flicked on the shower and immediately stood under the stream of as yet cold water, his mind too agitated to care that his body was protesting.

As the water pounded his scalp he closed his eyes and cursed silently. He felt as though he was drowning in emotions. Drowning in feelings he didn't want to have. Drowning in how mind-blowing last night had been. And not just physically.

Making love to Aideen had been different from anything he had ever experienced. At once he'd wanted to cherish her, protect her, possess her. In the act of love-making last night he had wanted their hearts and minds to fuse together as much as he had wanted their bodies to join. He had felt emotionally wrecked after it. As though he had exposed every part of himself to her.

Had he just made the biggest mistake of his life? He had never opened himself up to another person so much. He wasn't sure how to manage the vulnerability of that. And now she was saying she wanted it never to end.

Part of him understood that. God knew it felt so good, so right, to have her by his side. He drew strength from her. From her enthusiasm, from her sense of fun, and also from her quiet compassion.

But he couldn't ever commit to a relationship. Not with its demands and hurts and misunderstandings. Not when he already lost all those he had loved. What if he messed up in years to come and lost her? Just as he'd messed up with Orla? What if he failed her as he'd failed his mum and dad?

He was no good at relationships. In the end he would only hurt her. He didn't even know what to say to her now.

When she heard the bathroom door close Aideen looked down at her trembling hands and drew in a shaky breath. What had just happened?

She had spoken the truth—that was what had happened. And she had got it all wrong.

After last night she'd thought he might feel the same way. Even this morning, when he had looked at her with such affection, she'd thought there was more to this for him than just a casual affair.

Oh, God, she was so bad at reading men. First Ed. Now Patrick. How could she have got it so wrong?

He had looked horrified when she'd said she wanted it to last for ever. She had said it unconsciously. But it had been the truth.

Humiliation burnt deep in her stomach and her heart pounded in her chest. She needed to get out of here before he returned to the bedroom.

She wrapped the sheet about her and frantically picked her clothes off the bedroom floor. And then she ran down the ornate corridor to her own bedroom.

There, she collapsed on to the bed, her pulse pounding, her entire body trembling. Her skin was burning with embarrassment, but ice was flowing through her veins.

What was she going to do? She had sworn she would never fall for a man again, and here she was in love with a billionaire who was completely out of her league. A man who had run at the first notion of her wanting more from their relationship.

What had she been *thinking*? Talk about messing up on a spectacular scale.

She needed to get away. The humiliation was too much. She couldn't stay here. She couldn't pretend not to have feelings for him.

She winced at the thought of walking away. It might mean never seeing him again. Was she really ready for that? No. But there was no alternative.

An hour later, after an extra-long shower and generally delaying as long as she could, she walked downstairs. Patrick was nowhere to be seen, so she grabbed a cup of coffee, wrestling once again with the machine, and sat at the island unit, all the while rehearsing what she was going to say to him.

Not long afterwards he arrived in the kitchen, dressed in a slim-fitting navy suit. It showed the contours of his broad-shouldered, narrow-hipped frame to perfection, and for a crazy moment she longed to go to him, to wrap her arms about his waist, lower her forehead to that impregnable masculine strength and the power of his chest. Longed to inhale him. Soap… The sweet, musky tang of his skin…

He had no right to look so gorgeous and calm when she felt so distraught. But his calmness strengthened her conviction that she was going to leave here with her dignity intact.

He glanced at his watch. 'I have another conference call in ten minutes and then some meetings in Paris later. When I get back I think we should speak.'

His tone, his words, his stance were all shutting her out. He barely looked at her. Where had the warm and kind man of last night gone? Had it all been an act?

Horrible tension filled the room. Unsaid words, hurt and humiliation were thick in the air.

She wanted things to go back to where they'd been when they had woken, or to last night. To that carefree existence where reality had been suspended.

She didn't know what he was thinking. And the vulnerability that came with that cut her to the core.

Did he regret their relationship? Did he even regret answering the door to her that night of the storm? Did he wish she had never come into his life?

He was waiting for her to say something, but her throat was closed over and she was struggling to tell him what she had rehearsed. It was as though her heart was physically preventing her from saying the words logic said she had to speak.

He came a little closer and leant a hand against the island unit, his voice less brisk now, almost sad. 'I've always told you that I never want to be in a permanent relationship. I've never lied to you, Aideen.'

First Ed had cheated on her. Now Patrick looked as though he wanted to head for the hills. She had to understand why she wasn't good enough...why she kept getting relationships wrong.

'Why don't you want to be in a relationship?'

He looked totally taken aback by her question for a while, and then frustration flared on his face. 'I'm not interested...I don't want to be tied down. I want to be able to focus on work. It's not something I've ever wanted in life.'

Was it really that simple for him? Maybe it was. Maybe he didn't need love or affection.

She couldn't think straight.

Swallowing deeply, she said in a strained voice, 'I think we should call a stop to it all…it's becoming too complicated.'

A slash of red appeared on his cheeks and his voice was cool when he spoke. 'I don't want it to end, but if that's what you wish…'

Why couldn't he fight her a little? Had last night been nothing but a figment of her imagination?

She had to pull herself together.

All along she had said this would never work, and yet after just one night in his bed she had become delusional.

Now she knew for certain that this was never going to work. That this had been nothing but a brief interlude in her life. A magical, unbelievable interlude, but one that had to end. This wasn't her world. She didn't belong here.

She stood up and placed her cup in the dishwasher before turning to him. 'I think it would be best if I leave now.'

He moved closer to her, his hands landing on his hips. 'Oh, come on, Aideen. There's no need for this. Stay. I don't want you to go. Why can't we just enjoy each other's company for a while?'

'I'm not up for a casual relationship, Patrick.'

He looked at her in exasperation. 'Fine. I'll respect that. Nothing needs to happen between us again. You don't even have a home to go to. The cottage isn't ready.'

'I'll sort something out.'

'Stay at Ashbrooke.'

'You're not getting it, are you?'

'What do you mean?'

The sheer overwhelming impact of standing so close to his powerful, addictive frame but being so adrift from him emotionally had her blurting out, 'I can't stay in Ashbrooke. I can't be around you, Patrick.'

Heat fired through her body. Her cheeks were red-hot and tears burnt at the back of her eyes. She had said too much already, but she couldn't hold back the truth. The weight of it was physically hurting her chest.

'For the simple reason that I've fallen in love with you.'

Without meaning to do so he stepped back from her.

This was all going wrong.

She wasn't supposed to be telling him she loved him.

He didn't know what to say.

And in that moment he regretted ever opening up to Aideen. He should have kept his distance. He shouldn't have let her in. Look at what had happened as a result. He'd said he didn't want to hurt her. Judging by the pained expression on her face, he had done exactly that.

'I never wanted to hurt you.'

She gave a little laugh. 'I'm sure I'll get over it.' She paused and then stood up a little straighter, looked him in the eye. 'It was never going to work anyway. I always knew that. We are from different worlds. I don't belong in this world of wealth. I want a relationship of equals— one where I bring the same as the other person. That was never going to be the case with us.'

Though she looked as though she might crumble, she gave him a wobbly smile, her eyes brimming with tears again.

With a light shrug she added, 'This was never going

to be anything more than a brief interlude of happy madness. And even though I can barely breathe right now, knowing it's over, in my heart I know I will always cherish these weeks together. I'm glad I met you. And a part of me will always love you.'

Pain and shock had him sitting there and watching her walk away. He couldn't take it in, process all that she had said.

Both of them were agreeing that being together wouldn't work.

But if that was the case why did it feel as though he was being torn apart?

Less than ten minutes later he was still trying to process all that had happened when she reappeared in the kitchen, her suitcase beside her.

'I've booked a flight back to Ireland. When you return to Ashbrooke can you bring my files and paperwork from the orangery? I haven't had time to pack them. Perhaps you can ask one of your staff to do so?'

'I'll ask William to drop them off at the cottage.'

Part of him wanted to plead with her to stay. But this was for the best. Everything had spiralled out of control. He couldn't give Aideen the type of relationship she needed and deserved.

'I'll organise for my plane to take you.'

'No! Absolutely not.'

He was about to fight her, but then he realised why she would feel the need to pay for her own transport home.

With a resigned shrug of acceptance he said, 'I'll drop you to the airport.'

'I've already asked Bernard to take me.'

Fury shot through him and he said abruptly, 'No. *I'm* taking you.'

He had hurt her and let her down. The least he could do was see her safely to the airport. Say goodbye somewhere other than in the house where they had made love.

She looked away for a few seconds, and when she spoke again, he was taken aback by the pain in her voice.

'No. Bernard is taking me.' Tears shone in her eyes. 'I just want to go.'

'Aideen...'

Angry eyes flicked to his, and her voice was raw with emotion. 'I don't understand why you're fighting me on this. I can see that deep down you want me to go.'

'That's not true.'

'Yes, it is. You fled from our bed this morning. You're distancing yourself from me—burying yourself in work. Admit it, Patrick, you're pushing me away. Like you push everyone away.'

'I have never pretended that my work doesn't come first. It has to.'

'Oh, *please*... No, it doesn't. You just want it that way. At least admit that much to yourself.' She stopped and closed her eyes for a few seconds. When she reopened them they were filled with pain. 'Bernard will drive me to the airport.'

'I want to—'

She cut across him. 'Please don't make this any harder for me. I'm humiliated enough.'

He reached for her. Anger at his own bungling of this situation had him saying sharply, 'You have no reason to feel humiliated. I should never have suggested you come to Paris. This was all a mistake on my part. I'm sorry that I hurt you. That you have these feelings for me. But

I can't reciprocate them. Not with you. Not with anyone. I don't deserve your love, Aideen. Please remember that.'

She yanked her arm free and strode away from him.

He followed her out to the front steps, but she was already getting into the waiting car. Not once did she look back towards him.

CHAPTER ELEVEN

CYCLING HOME FROM MOONCOYNE, her front basket sparsely filled with the few food items she had forced herself to buy at the weekly farmers' market in the hope that they might kick-start her appetite again, Aideen heard the low cooing of a wood pigeon. Something about its regular familiar call reassured her. It told her that the world went on spinning even though it felt as though hers had ground to a halt.

Spring was in full bloom. The trees that lined the road were no longer stark grey-brown statues, reaching up to the sky, but lush green flowing bodies of movement and life. Waves of white cow parsley littered the hedgerows on either side of her, yellow buttercup flowers popping through at intervals.

Everything was changing.

It had been a week since she had returned from Paris. She had moved back into Fuchsia Cottage immediately, not caring about the dust or the noise as the builders carried out the renovations. It wasn't as if she was getting a lot of work done anyway. Thankfully their work was due to be completed by the end of next week. Hopefully then she would be able to give her work one hundred per cent of her concentration.

She had neither seen nor heard from Patrick since she'd returned. A part of her had hoped he might contact her. See how she was doing. Which was pretty crazy, really. He was probably just relieved to move on from what had been a disastrous scenario from his point of view.

He had visibly paled when she'd said she loved him. The panic in his eyes had told her everything she needed to know. Even now her cheeks glowed bright red at that memory.

In her first days at home she had wondered if she had made the worst decision of her life, becoming so involved, so intimate with him. In those long days and sleepless nights she had lived with numbing pain and an overwhelming sense of loss. And the haunting question as to whether her judgement had been all wrong once again.

But in the days that had followed, as her initial shock and gruelling pain had subsided a little, she'd found a clarity of thinking that had evaded her all the time she was with him.

She had been so overpowered, intrigued, in love with him, that when they'd been together she hadn't been able to think straight, think objectively.

Being with him had been like being awash with emotions that left no room for perspective. A perspective that now told her that it could never have lasted. He had said from the outset that he didn't want to be in a relationship. And she knew only too well that they were from different worlds. But when she had been with him all she had known was desire, longing, excitement, happiness. An itch to bury herself into his very soul, to know him better than she even knew herself.

Now that she was away from him, those emotions had lessened and she had finally got that perspective. Though her heart was physically sore, though she could barely eat or sleep, and though she sometimes thought she was going mad with her frustration, her wanting to be near him again, she didn't regret anything.

How could she when she had experienced such intense love and passion for another person?

Yes, she had wanted it to be for ever. She hadn't wanted it to end. But better that than never to have experienced it at all. How incredibly sad it would be to live a life never knowing such love existed.

In her heart she knew he had loved her in his own way. She had seen it shining in his eyes when they had made love. In the things he had whispered to her. But he hadn't loved her enough. And that was a fact she would have to learn to live with.

Now she had to start focusing on her work again. And hope that with time the pain would subside.

She neared the junction for the turning down to the road that led to her cottage and her pulse speeded up as she passed the wide entrance to his estate. But then she brought her bike to a sudden wobbly stop.

She dismounted, turned, and stared back at the board that had appeared on the wall. A sales board, to be precise, for a prestigious Dublin firm of auctioneers. And written on it, in giant capital letters, were the words FOR SALE: Historic House and Thousand-Acre Estate.

He was selling Ashbrooke!

What was he thinking?

She knew how much he loved this estate. Was he so desperate to put distance between himself and her?

She wheeled her bike over to the imposing twenty-foot wrought-iron double gates. For a minute she considered the intercom. Should she just leave it? It was none of her business, after all. But she could not shake off the feeling that he was selling for all the wrong reasons.

She pressed down on the buzzer and jumped when it was quickly answered. She instantly recognised his housekeeper's voice.

'Hi, Maureen, it's Aideen Ryan. I want to have a word with Patrick.'

'Aideen? Of course—come on in. I'll give Patrick a call to let him know you're here.'

The gates opened slowly and Aideen drew in a deep breath before she jumped back on her bike and started to cycle up the drive.

When she caught her first glimpse of the house, in all its magnificent grandeur, her chest tightened with a heaviness that barely allowed her to breathe. How could he walk away from this house which meant so much to him? She tried to imagine someone else living here but it seemed impossible.

The sound of fast-approaching horse's hooves on the drive behind her had her wobbling on her bike once again, and she came to an ungraceful stop when she hit the grass verge.

She twisted around to see Patrick, heading in her direction riding a horse. He was a natural horseman, confident and assured. Totally in control. And heartbreakingly gorgeous.

He pulled the horse to a stop a few feet away.

Heat and desire instantly coiled between them. Her heart thumped wildly against her chest as his eyes held her captive.

Memory snapshots of him making love to her had her almost crying out in pain, and she gripped the handlebars of the bike tighter against the tremble in her legs.

He dismounted and led his horse towards her. He was wearing a loose blue shirt over his jodhpurs. His eyes matched the blue of the sky behind him, but gave nothing away as to what he was thinking.

'Maureen rang to say you wanted to speak to me.'

No, *How are you? How have you been?* Instead this bleak, unwelcoming comment. It made her feel as though all the closeness and warmth they had once shared had been nothing but a mirage.

She couldn't show him how upset she felt, so she took a deep breath and tried to control her voice. 'I saw the for-sale sign.'

He frowned slightly and shrugged. 'And?'

'Why are you selling?'

'I listened to what you said. You're right. I *am* isolated here in Ashbrooke.'

She didn't understand. Bewildered, she asked, 'Where are you going to go?'

'Wherever my work takes me. I have property throughout the world. I'll move around as necessary.'

'But you *love* Ashbrooke, Patrick. I know you do. You love this house and this land as though you were born into it.'

His mouth twisted unhappily and he fixed her with a lancing glare. 'I thought you would be pleased. It was you who put the idea in my head.'

'No. My point was that you deliberately choose houses that enable you to be isolated. But you can be isolated in the middle of Manhattan if you really want to. I didn't mean for you to sell Ashbrooke. This is crazy.'

'I need to move on. It's nothing more complicated than that.'

'Isn't it? Are you sure our relationship hasn't anything

to do with it? Are you worried I might still hope something can happen between us? Because if that's the case, please believe me—I have absolutely no expectations. I know it's over. And I accept it's for the best. Never the twain shall meet, after all.'

He shook his head angrily and uttered a low curse. In that moment he looked exhausted. 'Aideen, I wish I could explain...but I can't.'

What did he mean? For a moment she considered him, wanting to ask what there was to explain. It was all pretty simple, after all. He didn't love her. End of story.

'Please reconsider selling Ashbrooke. Moving from here won't change anything. Selling a house won't stop you being isolated. You need to open your heart to others. My fear is that you won't, and you'll be alone for the rest of your life. And you deserve more than that.'

He threw her a furious look. 'Do I really, though? I hurt Orla. I hurt you. Why on earth are you saying that I deserve more?'

'Because you're a good man, Patrick.'

His hands tightened on the reins. 'And you're too kind-hearted and generous.'

She lifted her chin and glared at him. 'Don't patronise me. I know what I'm talking about. And maybe you should listen to your own advice sometimes. You told me once that I should believe in myself. Well, maybe you should do the same.'

His jaw clenched. 'I can't give you what you need, Aideen.'

'This isn't about me. Trust me—I wouldn't be here if I hadn't seen the for-sale sign. I want nothing from you. But I'm not going to let you make the mistake of selling the house you love because for once you actually allowed someone into your life.'

His eyes were sharp, angry shards of blue ice. 'That has nothing to do with it.'

'Are you sure? Because I'm not convinced. Are you going to reconnect with Orla and your friends once you leave Ashbrooke? What changes are you going to make to your life?'

His mouth thinned and he threw her a blistering look. 'Frankly, that's none of your business.'

She gave a tight laugh of shock and took a step back. Her heart went into a freefall of despondency. 'Wow, you *really* know how to put a person in her place.' Her throat was tight, but she forced herself to speak. 'And it *is* my business because I care for you. I don't want to see you shutting more and more people out of your life. You deserve to be happy in life, Patrick. Remember that.'

There was nothing else she could say. She turned and picked up her bike. At the same time his phone rang.

He gave another low curse and muttered, 'This number has been calling me non-stop all morning.'

As she pushed away she heard him answer it.

She pedalled furiously.

Seeing him again had brought home just how much she missed him. Would she ever meet another man to whom she was so physically attracted? Just from standing close to him her body was on fire. And her heart felt as though it was in pieces. Because emotionally she missed him twice as much. She wanted him in her life. It was against all logic and reason. But there it was. She wanted his intelligence, his kindness, his strength.

The sound of his voice calling her and the thundering of hooves had her looking around, startled. Patrick was racing towards her. He yanked his horse to a stop, but didn't dismount. He looked aghast.

'That was a hospital in Dublin calling. Orla has gone into early labour.'

For a moment she wondered why he was telling her, but then she saw the fear in his eyes. He didn't know what to do.

She dropped her bike down on the grass verge. 'Are you going to go to Dublin to be with her?'

He looked pale and drawn. For a moment she thought he hadn't heard her question. But then he looked down at her beseechingly. 'I don't know what to do. I don't want to cause her any upset.'

'Did she tell the hospital to call you and ask you to come?'

'Yes.'

'Well, then, she needs you.' For a moment she looked at the horse warily, and then she held out her hand to Patrick. 'Pull me up. We need to get back to the house quickly. While you get changed I'll organise for your helicopter to come and collect you.'

He looked at her, taken aback, but then nodded his agreement. 'Put your leg in the stirrup and I'll pull you up.'

He drew her up and sat her in front of him. It was her first time on a horse, and it looked like a long, long way down, but she couldn't think of that. Instead she tried to think of the practical arrangements that needed to be sorted out in order to get Patrick to Dublin immediately. She tried to ignore how good it felt to be so physically close to him again.

At the stables, a groom helped her dismount. When Patrick jumped off he hesitated, so she held his hand in hers and tugged him forward. 'Come on—there's no time to waste.'

They entered the kitchen via the cloakroom. 'Is the number for your pilot stored on your phone?'

'Yes, but I'm not—'

'No, Patrick. You *have* to go. Orla has never needed you more than now. I know you feel you have failed her in the past. That there is a lot of hurt and misunderstanding. But right now none of that matters. Orla and her baby are the only things that matter. She needs her brother. She needs your strength and support.'

For a moment he blinked, but then, as her words finally registered, determination came back into his eyes. 'You're right. Call the helicopter. I'll be ready in ten minutes.'

Aideen immediately made the call, and the helicopter crew promised to be at Ashbrooke within twenty minutes. True to his word, Patrick was back in the kitchen within ten. Wearing a dark red polo shirt and faded denim jeans, his hair still wet from the shower, he looked gorgeous—if a little distracted. She could feel the pumped-up energy radiating from him. She needed to keep him calm, reassure him.

'The helicopter will be here in ten minutes. Do you want to call the hospital again for an update?'

Instantly he took the phone from the counter and dialled the number. He spoke looking out through the glass extension, down towards the sea, his polo shirt pulled tight across his wide shoulders, his jeans hugging his hips, and Aideen remembered her first night here. How in awe of him she'd been. How bowled over she'd been by his good looks.

Her heart dropped with a thud and she felt physical

pain in her chest. Would she ever stop missing him every single second of every single minute of every single hour?

'She's seven centimetres dilated…whatever that means. She's doing okay, but they're worried as she's a month early.' His jaw working, he added, 'She has nobody with her. Damn it, she shouldn't be alone at a time like this.'

She walked towards him and placed a hand on his arm. 'She's going to be okay. She's in good hands, but she'll be relieved to see you. I bet it's pretty lonely, going through something so big all on your own.'

He inhaled a deep breath at her words and felt some of the tension leave his body.

'You're right.'

And then it hit him just how much he wanted Aideen by his side today. He felt as though he had been struck by lightning, the realisation was so startling.

'Come to Dublin with me.'

'No, I can't…'

'I want you to come—please.' His throat worked. Could he actually say the words he needed to say? After so many years of going it alone, to ask for help felt alien. 'I need your support.'

Aideen looked totally taken aback. Out of the window he could see the helicopter approaching. He looked from it to her, beseechingly.

'Okay, I'll come.'

He was about to lead her out to the garden when he remembered something. 'Hold on for a minute. There's something I need to bring.'

He sprinted down to his office and then straight back to the kitchen.

Aideen looked at the memory chest and then up at

him. She said nothing, but there were tears in her eyes before she looked away from him.

As the helicopter took off his pilot gave them their estimated flight time. He inhaled a frustrated breath and shook his head.

Beside him, Aideen asked, 'Are you okay?'

'No. If Orla had told me she was back in Dublin I could have been there much earlier. I wouldn't have been ignoring my phone all morning.'

'I can understand your frustration, but Orla wasn't to know that she was going to go into early labour. And, anyway, that was *her* decision. She's a grown woman, Patrick, about to have her own child. You can't control everything in your life. Today you just need to be there for Orla. Be the brother she loves, and trust that that's enough.'

Thrown, he was about to argue. But then he realised she was right. He had to stop thinking that the only way he could show his love for Orla was by taking charge and forcing her to lead the life he thought she should.

With a small smile he lifted his hands in admission and said, 'You're right.'

She gave him a smile in return and then looked away, her gaze on the endless patchwork of green fields that appeared through the window as the pilot banked the helicopter.

He longed to reach out and touch her, to hold her hand in his. His heart felt as though it would pound right out of his chest at any moment. Being so near to her but not being able to touch her was torture. But the hurt in her eyes was even worse. You could cut the tension in the helicopter with a knife.

Though his teeth were clenched tight, he forced them apart in order to speak. 'How is your cottage?'

She glanced at him warily, as though questioning why he was asking. 'Dusty and noisy…' She paused and held his gaze. 'But that doesn't matter. It's just really good to be home.' Then her gaze flicked away.

Why was the silence between them making him feel so uncomfortable? Before, he'd never had an issue with silence, but now it felt as if his heart was being ripped out to fill the void that sat like a physical entity between them.

He had to speak. Anything but this mocking silence which drove home much too eloquently everything he had lost: her humour, her warmth, her spark and her love of life.

'William will bring down all your files and office equipment once the cottage is finished.'

She nodded to this, her face impassive. But then she looked towards him with a frown. 'What's going to happen to William and Maureen and the rest of the staff?'

'It's part of my sale conditions that all the existing staff are retained by the new owner.'

'They're going to miss you—they're really fond of you.'

Were they? He had never stopped to think about it. But now he realised just how much he would miss them, too.

What was he *doing*? Was anything making sense in his life any more?

He looked back at her when he heard her clear her throat. 'I really hope your time with Orla goes well today. Please be patient. I bet Orla misses you desperately, but can't say it. Maybe for the same reasons that you can't say it to her.'

His mind raced at her words. Did Orla fear losing him, too? Was that why she always pushed him away? No wonder the harder he tried, the harder she pushed back.

He looked at Aideen in amazement. 'You might be right. So I just need to be there for her?'

'Yes!' With a small laugh she added, 'And for goodness' sake don't go ordering the midwives and doctors about. I'm sure they know what they are doing.'

'I won't.' He gave her a rueful look and added, 'My managing directors have a lot to thank you for, by the way. I thought about what you said about delegating more control to them and I've started doing so.'

She gave a small satisfied smile. 'And I bet the world hasn't come crashing down, has it?'

He gave an eye-roll. 'It's actually a relief to not be bogged down in day-to-day operations. I now have more time to focus on a strategic level.'

He paused for a minute, uncertain of where to take the conversation. There was so much more he should say, but he couldn't find the right words.

'How about you? What are your plans?'

For a split second she winced, but then she sat up in her seat, her voice unwavering as she spoke. 'I've had a lot of orders since Paris, and more than ever I'm determined to make Little Fire the most exciting bespoke textile design business in the world. And I'm looking forward to getting to know the people of Mooncoyne, I want to become part of the community. Get involved. I want to establish roots, to belong.'

Fresh admiration for her determination to succeed washed over him. But then a kick of reality came when it dawned on him that he didn't feature in any of her plans.

Which was only to be expected. And yet it twisted in his gut that they would soon go their separate ways.

It was what he wanted. What they had to do. Wasn't it?

CHAPTER TWELVE

HIS HELICOPTER LANDED on the hospital's helipad and within minutes they were rushing through the front doors of the hospital.

The receptionist at the front desk blushed furiously when she looked up to see Patrick, and garbled out directions to the delivery ward. As she left Aideen gave her an understanding smile. He had that effect on all women. Herself included.

He didn't wait for the lifts but instead took the steps up to the third floor two at a time. Aideen followed his frantic pace, glad she was fit from cycling around Mooncoyne.

Again there was a flutter of activity when he stopped at the nurses' desk. Then they were directed to a number of chairs dotted along the corridor outside the delivery rooms, while one of the nurses went into the delivery suite to enquire if Orla was able to see him.

She could feel Patrick's nervousness radiating off him. 'It's going to be okay.'

He looked at her for a long while and then nodded, the tension in his face easing a little.

The door of the delivery suite opened and the nurse came back out, beaming. 'They're ready for you,' she said.

Patrick looked at Aideen in amazement. 'Does that mean that…that the baby has been born already?'

Memories of holding her own niece for the first time, the tremendous wave of love that had speared her heart, caused a lump of happiness to form in Aideen's throat. 'Yes. You better get in there.'

'Will you come in with me?'

'No. This is *your* time with Orla and her baby.'

He hesitated for a moment. 'What if I say the wrong thing?'

'You won't. Just be yourself… And remember Orla is a mum now, well capable of looking after herself. She doesn't need you to make decisions for her—she just needs your support.' She paused and eyed him with amusement. 'And advice… But only if she asks for it.'

'Will you wait here for me? I'd like to introduce you to Orla.'

'I'll wait.'

He stood and moved to the door, but then turned and said, 'Thank you. For everything.'

She returned his smile, but after the door had swung closed after him it slowly faded.

From the delivery suite she could hear the murmur of voices. Earnest, but with no hint of argument. Maybe they would be okay. She willed them to be kind and patient with one another. To realise that they needed each other. She hoped they could forget the past and realise what a wonderful future they had before them.

Patrick would be a great uncle. He had so much generosity and integrity burning inside him. Along with strength and pride. He would be an incredible role model for Orla's baby.

The murmurs had given way to light laughter. Patrick now had a newly expanded family to fill his life.

It was time for her to move on.

She left a brief note for him on her chair, and then walked back down the stairs and out of the hospital. She would get a cab to the train station. In Cork, she would get a bus to Mooncoyne.

As she queued at the taxi rank she tried to ignore the excited families going in and out of the hospital. But when a young couple emerged, the dad proudly holding his newborn child, she had to turn away, tears filming her eyes. She could go and stay with her own family, here in Dublin, but knew that if she saw her mum she would instantly burst into tears.

She would go home and lose herself in her work.

The taxi rank was busy and the line shuffled along slowly. With growing impatience she willed the taxis to come. She needed to get home. She needed to be in Mooncoyne. She needed the silence and beauty of West Cork in order to heal her broken heart.

At last it was her turn. The taxi drew to a halt, but just as she stepped forward to open the rear door a hand clasped her arm.

Patrick.

She had been crying. He tried to draw in a deep breath, but his heart was pounding too loudly, his stomach flipping so frantically there simply wasn't enough room for his lungs to expand. He'd panicked when he had realised she had gone, and her note hadn't helped. She had said she wished him well, but would prefer it if he didn't contact her again.

This was going to be the most important conversation of his life.

What if he messed up?

What if he failed to convince her?

For a moment he hesitated, fearful of blowing this.

He had to pull himself together.

'Will you come for a walk with me?'

She looked back at the taxi and for a moment he thought she was going say no. But then her shoulders dropped and the wariness of her gaze lessened.

'Is this a good idea?'

He gave her a crooked smile and shrugged. 'I'm hoping it's the best idea I ever had.'

She stared at him in confusion, but then a faint hint of amusement shone in her eyes. 'Okay.'

He took her to a nearby park, where sunlight glimmered through the trees and cast dark dancing shadows on the grey tarmacadam paths.

He didn't know where to start, so he just blurted out everything that had been building in his chest, in his mind, in his heart, for the past week.

'I've missed you.'

She looked at him with surprise and hurt.

God, this was harder than he'd thought. He wanted her to understand but he couldn't find the words. He was usually articulate, forceful. But all of that was now lost to him.

Should he just take her into his arms and kiss her? Physically show her what he was trying to say?

That wasn't the answer.

He needed to start making things right.

'I'm sorry for what happened in Paris.'

Her head whipped round. In a rush, she said, 'No, *I*

should apologise. I said things that were too intense.' Pointing to the cute blush on her cheeks she added, 'As you can see, I'm pretty embarrassed about it all. I didn't mean to put you under any pressure. I guess I misread all the signs.'

He shook his head. 'No, you weren't to blame. Everything happened so quickly. The intensity of it all got to me. After focusing on nothing but work for so long I felt overwhelmed.'

Her mouth twisted ruefully. 'I guess what I said would have had most guys heading for the hills.'

A heavy sadness sat in his chest and his throat tightened with emotion. 'Not if they'd experienced what we had together. It was special... But I had believed for so long that I wasn't cut out to be in a relationship I couldn't see beyond that.'

She looked at him, bewildered. 'I don't know why you keep saying that you aren't suited to be in a relationship. Forget me, for one moment, and what we had. All I can see before me is a thoughtful, strong, honourable man who is deserving of love.' She shook her head in exasperation. 'You deserve to be loved, Patrick. I just hope in the future you can learn to let people into your life.'

He inhaled a steadying breath. He needed to let his heart speak and ignore the vulnerability and fear of exposing himself. The fear that she would say no.

'You asked me in Paris why I couldn't be in a relationship and I didn't answer you truthfully. It was a step I just couldn't take. Even now it feels like I'm about to yank out my heart and give it to you...which makes me feel pretty exposed.'

She looked at him, confused.

He took a deep breath.

'When Orla moved in with me I was frightened of losing her, like I'd lost my mum and dad. So I tried to protect her as best I could. But now, because of you, I understand that I took the wrong approach. I shouldn't have been so controlling, so protective. I should have included her in the decisions that had to be taken in the new life we were both suddenly facing.'

He inhaled a deep breath against the way his insides were tumbling.

'You were right about Orla. I have to let her decide what support she wants from me. I'll admit it will be hard to change, after years of trying to take charge, but I know I can no longer foist what I *think* she needs on her.'

His chest felt heavy with so many words still unsaid. He drew her away from the path and guided her to a bench under a giant chestnut tree. The wood was warm under his hands when he gripped the base of the seat tight. He glanced at her, and then away.

'That fear of losing someone is the reason why I swore I never wanted to be in love with a woman. In Paris, as we grew closer, that fear intensified. I was worried that if I fell in love with you I'd only end up losing you at some point in the future. And that thought terrified me.'

His jaw ached with tension and he had to work it loose before he continued.

'And rather than face that fear I refused to acknowledge what you meant to me. After we slept together all my feelings for you were exposed, and I panicked. I couldn't handle how I was feeling. How close I felt to you, how I wanted you in my life. And when you said you were leaving I didn't know how to ask you to stay.' Shaking his head, he added, 'At first I was angry at you for going. I wanted you not to love me.'

He gave a rueful laugh and looked towards the sky in disbelief.

'I was cross that you had fallen in love with me. As if somebody can opt in or out of falling in love. And then I tried to convince myself that perhaps you going was for the best. That if you stayed any longer I wouldn't be able to hide my feelings for you. And then I realised I was kidding myself—that I was lost without you. I missed you, Aideen, with every fibre of my being.'

He risked a quick glance in her direction and her look of compassion caught him off-guard. His throat tightened, but he forced himself to speak.

'For so long I thought I'd failed not only Orla but my mum and dad, too. That I had not faced up to my responsibilities. But now I realise I have to accept that I did the best I could in looking after Orla. That I couldn't do any more. I have to stop blaming myself.'

His heart raced in his chest and he squeezed his hands even tighter on the edge of the seat before he continued.

'Today, as Orla and I spoke, I could see for the first time in a very long time that we can have a relationship that works, one that's supportive and loving. And I realised that I have to stop worrying that I will mess up relationships... I have to let go of my fear of losing those I love. I also realised that if I let you go then I would really have failed. Failed you. And myself.'

Tears shone brightly in her eyes and his hand rose to capture her face. His thumb slowly stroked her skin. She was about to say something, but he spoke first.

'That first time I opened my door to you the night of the storm—when you fell into my arms and soaked me through—I looked into those startled brown eyes and deep inside myself I recognised you. Recognised that you are the one. But I was too wrapped up in feelings of guilt and fear to see it. The last thing I wanted to do was hurt you, so I kept telling myself not to fall for you. I hadn't reckoned on how you would worm your way into my heart. How my resilience would waver each time you smiled and laughed. I hadn't reckoned on the joy and fun you brought into my life. Just how mind-blowingly and crazily I would be physically attracted to you. How I'd lose my mind and my heart to you when we made love.'

His hand dropped from her cheek to hold hers. Blood pounded in his ears.

'I love you, Aideen. I don't know how, but in a matter of weeks you've turned my life upside down. I can't even pinpoint when I fell in love with you. Perhaps it was at every moment that you challenged me, whether it was on the tennis court or in how I chose to spend my life. Of course I didn't want to listen to you, but you loosened yet another chink in the armour I had wrapped around myself for years. Or maybe it was after I saw your delight went we ate at my club next to the Eiffel Tower. Until the day I die I will remember just how stunningly beautiful you looked that night.'

He watched her shocked expression, saw her hand pressed to her mouth. His stomach clenched.

He leant towards her and said in a low voice, 'Since Paris, all I can think of is our lovemaking...your soft whispers. I'm in love with you, Aideen Ryan.'

She said nothing, just shook her head, her hand still over her mouth. Didn't she believe him? Panic gripped him. Should he just stop? No. He had to tell her how much he loved her. How much he needed her in his life.

'I'm in love with your chocolate eyes, your smiling mouth, your messy chatterbox ways. There's so much I

want to know about you. How you like to celebrate Hal-
loween, Christmas, birthdays. What's your favourite fla-
vour of ice cream? There's so much I want to experience
with you. So much more I want to learn about you and fall
in love with. To go along with how much I love your lips.
The never-ending length of your eyelashes. Your constant
daydreaming. The five tiny piercings in your right ear.'

That, at least, elicited a smile.

'In Paris I was convinced I couldn't give you the love
you deserve. You had been hurt enough in the past without me adding to it. For so long I allowed my fear of losing those close to me to push people away. I was certain
I wasn't capable of being in an effective relationship. I
was terrified of taking that blind leap of faith—of telling someone you love them and all the vulnerabilities
and uncertainties that go with that.'

He looked into her eyes, his heart thumping wildly.

'You helped bring Orla and her baby girl back into
my life. My life was pretty empty until you arrived into
it. My heart had shut down. I was tired of losing people
I loved. But you kick-started it with a bang within hours
of turning up in my life. That night of the storm I tried
to shut you out, but you kept worming your way in with
your warmth and humour.'

He shook his head and ran a hand through his hair.

'At first I thought helping you would be a good distraction from everything that was happening with Orla.
But, in truth, now I realise that I wanted to make up for
failing Orla so badly by helping you instead. I hadn't anticipated that it would actually be more about you helping
me. As each day passed you became a bigger and bigger part of my life...until now I can't imagine a life with
you. So much so that in the past week I couldn't settle to

anything. I grew increasingly restless, and the only way I could think of distracting myself was by taking to the road again, by selling Ashbrooke. But the truth is I can't live without you. You have made me want to live life again—fully. You are the most beautiful, courageous, kind, funny, and tender woman I have ever met and I want you in my life…for ever.'

Her head swam with all his words. It would be so easy to give in to her heart, give in to the chemistry and attraction that drew her like a magnet to him. She wanted nothing more than to spend every second of the rest of her life with him, to know every single inch of him.

But they were from different worlds, and no amount of love would change that.

'I don't know what to say. Oh, Patrick… You know how I feel for you, but this is never going to work. We're too different. We're not equals. I don't want to be in an unbalanced relationship.'

The pull of his hand on hers forced her to look back up at him. Gentle eyes held her gaze.

'What are you afraid of?'

Her pulse pounded at his question and her throat dried. 'That you will have power over me. That I will spend my life feeling inadequate, unequal, that I didn't contribute my fair share.'

He pulled her closer until there was only an inch separating them. His beautiful gaze held hers with such compassion and warmth tears trickled down her cheeks in response.

'Have I ever done any of those things to you? Made you feel like you aren't my equal?'

'No…'

'Do you trust me?'

Her heart burst forth with the truth and she answered resoundingly. 'Yes, I trust you.'

'Will you trust me when I say that we *are* equals? That we are both bringing different but equally important things to this relationship? You are bringing empathy, joy, creativity…and you brought my family back together. What could be more important than that? You have a love for me that no one else can ever give me. How can any of those things be of less importance than wealth?' Before she could answer he said quickly, 'You *do* love me, don't you?'

She struggled to speak against the wave of emotions that churned in her body. She squeezed his hands, needing to clutch on to his strength in order to carry on. 'I love you with all my heart. You are kind and generous. More handsome than any man deserves to be. You make me feel like the most special person in the world. When we made love I felt an intimacy, a love for you, that was so intense, so real…it was almost frightening. I love you so much… But you have so much wealth, and I have practically nothing… It doesn't seem right. And I'm so confused.'

For a while he simply looked at her, deep in thought. His eyes grew sombre and determined. 'Are you saying that if I lost all my money in the morning you wouldn't love me?'

'No! Of course not!'

And then she stopped as a satisfied smile broke on his lips.

'So what *are* you saying?'

For the longest while she just stared at him, unsure. She trusted him. He had never tried to control or dominate her with his wealth and power. And if he was penniless it wouldn't change her love for him.

'I suppose I'm saying that I'm a little scared and daunted by all this.'

His head tilted to the side and he said gently, 'Being in love is a little scary…but I promise I will never hurt you.'

'Are you scared?'

'Of course! I'm scared of being hurt, too—of you not loving me as much as I love you.'

'But that would be impossible.'

'Would it? Are you willing to take the risk and be with me? I love you. I want you by my side always. I want to wake to your smile, sleep with you in my arms. I want to care for you, protect you, argue with you, grow old with you. I want to share everything I have with you. Because in giving, in sharing everything I have with you, I hope you'll see it as an indication of how much I love you. And in accepting me, and all that I have, you can show me how much you love and trust me. That you are willing to share my life.'

He dropped to his knees on the path before her and she could do nothing but gape at him, open-mouthed.

'Before this year is out I want to stand before our families and friends and ask you. Aideen Ryan, for richer or poorer, will you marry me?'

Dizzy, she closed her eyes for a moment. The sun warmed her face as she turned it upwards and her hand swept away the tears on her cheeks. A fiery intensity beat in her heart.

The sun danced beneath her eyelids and when she dropped her head she opened her eyes to the pale blue Irish sky. The same glorious colour as his eyes, which she then turned to. Eyes filled with love…and a little apprehension.

She could barely speak, her pulse was pounding so hard. 'I never thought I could ever love someone as much as I love you. With you I feel complete…I feel secure. I can be the best that I am with you. The world is more beautiful, more exciting, more intense with you in it. So, yes, I would be honoured to be your wife, to spend the rest of my life with you.'

His hands wrapped about her face and he gently drew her to him. Her breath caught at the power of the joy and love shining in his eyes.

He spoke in a low whisper. 'It has taken me so long to find you…to allow love into my life. I'm never letting you out of my sight again. Promise me that we will never sleep a night apart. That you will come with me wherever I go.'

Her thumb traced the lines of his lips and she spoke with light, teasing laughter. 'I promise… I will follow you to the ends of this world. But I'm warning you: I want lots of children, so you'll have a lot of uncomfortable nights in hospital chairs.'

At that he stood, and looked down at her with stunned joy. Then he pulled her up and, holding her by the waist, swung her around and around.

When he stopped they were both breathless with laughter. And then his gaze darkened. 'How about we start trying straight away?'

She inched forward and brushed her lips against his. 'Good idea.'

And then she was lost to his strength, his warmth. His love.

EPILOGUE

Eight months later

As SHE STOOD outside the double doors to the entrance of Ashbrooke's ballroom Aideen's fingers trembled where she held on to her dad's arm.

Behind her, her cousin and bridesmaid Kate fussed with the train of her dress.

To one side of the hallway a huge fir tree from the estate was bedecked in twinkling white Christmas lights. Through the windows beyond, fat flakes of snow fluttered down to join the heavy carpet of snow that already covered the estate.

Tomorrow—Christmas Day—she would wake up beside her husband. Giddy excitement raced through her at the thought, and she smiled quietly to herself.

She ran a hand over the delicate lace of her dress, her trained eye once again inspecting it. But there was no need. It was perfect.

She had spent weeks deciding on the design, and it had been handcrafted by a group of lacemakers who lived locally. It was a traditional Bandon Lace design, but with personal touches added—the shields that represented valour and honour on the Fitzsimon family crest, the three griffins of the Ryan crest representing courage and bravery. A seashell to represent Ashbrooke House. The sailing boat from the Parisian coat of arms. Symbols from all the places where she had fallen deeper and deeper in love with Patrick.

And on her feet were the ivory ankle-strap sandals Mustard and Mayo had bought her all those months ago.

With a nod, she signalled to her dad that she was ready.

The doors opened and once again she was dazzled by the ornate heavy gilt mirrored walls, the cherub-filled frescoed ceiling of the ballroom, and her heart leapt at its spectacular beauty.

Her family and friends beamed back at her and her already bursting heart exploded with joy. Her mum openly cried, while her two brothers tried to pretend they weren't.

Orla, holding baby Evie in her arms, looked from Aideen to Patrick with love and pride.

Patrick's best man, Frédéric Forbin, whispered something to him and he nodded in response.

When was he going to turn to her?

The dogs sat patiently at his feet, both wearing pale pink bows to match the bridal party. Behind him stood his large group of friends, including Lord Balfe, all of whom had travelled from around the world to be here. Friends who were once again part of his life.

And then he turned to her.

She wanted to run to him but forced herself to take the slow bridal steps. His hair was shorn once again, highlighting the sharp masculine lines of his face, the brilliant blue of his eyes.

Step by step she moved closer to her best friend. To the

man who made her feel like the most beautiful woman in the world.

With him, she was complete.

Before him, she'd felt as though she was a feather—floating through the air, happy, but never quite belonging, never quite understanding.

And now, because of him, she understood. That this life was about love. Giving love. But also receiving it. That was all that really mattered.

And tonight, at the stroke of midnight, she would give him his Christmas present: the news that she was six weeks pregnant.

* * * * *

MILLS & BOON®
Hardback – February 2016

ROMANCE

Leonetti's Housekeeper Bride	Lynne Graham
The Surprise De Angelis Baby	Cathy Williams
Castelli's Virgin Widow	Caitlin Crews
The Consequence He Must Claim	Dani Collins
Helios Crowns His Mistress	Michelle Smart
Illicit Night with the Greek	Susanna Carr
The Sheikh's Pregnant Prisoner	Tara Pammi
A Deal Sealed by Passion	Louise Fuller
Saved by the CEO	Barbara Wallace
Pregnant with a Royal Baby!	Susan Meier
A Deal to Mend Their Marriage	Michelle Douglas
Swept into the Rich Man's World	Katrina Cudmore
His Shock Valentine's Proposal	Amy Ruttan
Craving Her Ex-Army Doc	Amy Ruttan
The Man She Could Never Forget	Meredith Webber
The Nurse Who Stole His Heart	Alison Roberts
Her Holiday Miracle	Joanna Neil
Discovering Dr Riley	Annie Claydon
His Forever Family	Sarah M. Anderson
How to Sleep with the Boss	Janice Maynard

MILLS & BOON®
Large Print – February 2016

ROMANCE

Claimed for Makarov's Baby	Sharon Kendrick
An Heir Fit for a King	Abby Green
The Wedding Night Debt	Cathy Williams
Seducing His Enemy's Daughter	Annie West
Reunited for the Billionaire's Legacy	Jennifer Hayward
Hidden in the Sheikh's Harem	Michelle Conder
Resisting the Sicilian Playboy	Amanda Cinelli
Soldier, Hero...Husband?	Cara Colter
Falling for Mr December	Kate Hardy
The Baby Who Saved Christmas	Alison Roberts
A Proposal Worth Millions	Sophie Pembroke

HISTORICAL

Christian Seaton: Duke of Danger	Carole Mortimer
The Soldier's Rebel Lover	Marguerite Kaye
Return of Scandal's Son	Janice Preston
The Forgotten Daughter	Lauri Robinson
No Conventional Miss	Eleanor Webster

MEDICAL

Hot Doc from Her Past	Tina Beckett
Surgeons, Rivals...Lovers	Amalie Berlin
Best Friend to Perfect Bride	Jennifer Taylor
Resisting Her Rebel Doc	Joanna Neil
A Baby to Bind Them	Susanne Hampton
Doctor...to Duchess?	Annie O'Neil

MILLS & BOON®
Hardback – March 2016

ROMANCE

The Italian's Ruthless Seduction	Miranda Lee
Awakened by Her Desert Captor	Abby Green
A Forbidden Temptation	Anne Mather
A Vow to Secure His Legacy	Annie West
Carrying the King's Pride	Jennifer Hayward
Bound to the Tuscan Billionaire	Susan Stephens
Required to Wear the Tycoon's Ring	Maggie Cox
The Secret That Shocked De Santis	Natalie Anderson
The Greek's Ready-Made Wife	Jennifer Faye
Crown Prince's Chosen Bride	Kandy Shepherd
Billionaire, Boss...Bridegroom?	Kate Hardy
Married for their Miracle Baby	Soraya Lane
The Socialite's Secret	Carol Marinelli
London's Most Eligible Doctor	Annie O'Neil
Saving Maddie's Baby	Marion Lennox
A Sheikh to Capture Her Heart	Meredith Webber
Breaking All Their Rules	Sue MacKay
One Life-Changing Night	Louisa Heaton
The CEO's Unexpected Child	Andrea Laurence
Snowbound with the Boss	Maureen Child

MILLS & BOON®
Large Print – March 2016

ROMANCE

A Christmas Vow of Seduction	Maisey Yates
Brazilian's Nine Months' Notice	Susan Stephens
The Sheikh's Christmas Conquest	Sharon Kendrick
Shackled to the Sheikh	Trish Morey
Unwrapping the Castelli Secret	Caitlin Crews
A Marriage Fit for a Sinner	Maya Blake
Larenzo's Christmas Baby	Kate Hewitt
His Lost-and-Found Bride	Scarlet Wilson
Housekeeper Under the Mistletoe	Cara Colter
Gift-Wrapped in Her Wedding Dress	Kandy Shepherd
The Prince's Christmas Vow	Jennifer Faye

HISTORICAL

His Housekeeper's Christmas Wish	Louise Allen
Temptation of a Governess	Sarah Mallory
The Demure Miss Manning	Amanda McCabe
Enticing Benedict Cole	Eliza Redgold
In the King's Service	Margaret Moore

MEDICAL

Falling at the Surgeon's Feet	Lucy Ryder
One Night in New York	Amy Ruttan
Daredevil, Doctor...Husband?	Alison Roberts
The Doctor She'd Never Forget	Annie Claydon
Reunited...in Paris!	Sue MacKay
French Fling to Forever	Karin Baine

MILLS & BOON®

Why shop at millsandboon.co.uk?

Each year, thousands of romance readers find their perfect read at millsandboon.co.uk. That's because we're passionate about bringing you the very best romantic fiction. Here are some of the advantages of shopping at www.millsandboon.co.uk:

* **Get new books first**—you'll be able to buy your favourite books one month before they hit the shops

* **Get exclusive discounts**—you'll also be able to buy our specially created monthly collections, with up to 50% off the RRP

* **Find your favourite authors**—latest news, interviews and new releases for all your favourite authors and series on our website, plus ideas for what to try next

* **Join in**—once you've bought your favourite books, don't forget to register with us to rate, review and join in the discussions

Visit **www.millsandboon.co.uk**
for all this and more today!☞